MW00761513

The Púca

Terri Squires

This is a work of fiction. Names, characters, businesses, places, events and incidents are either the products of the author's imagination or used in a fictitious manner. Any resemblance to actual persons, living or dead, or actual events is purely coincidental.

Acknowledgments

It's amazing to me. I can't believe it's been five years since I woke from a dream with a simple idea for a book, and a lot of what ifs.

What if I had two protagonists instead of one? What if they were twins, a boy and a girl? Many years later and dozens of drafts later, here is my novel.

But no writer can work alone. We all need the help and support of our family and friends. I'd like to thank my sister Darlene, my son Scott, and my mom Mikey for being my sounding boards. To my cousin Jessica, a special thank you for being my first fan of the roughest fifty pages anyone has ever seen.

For my professors at Stony Brook University, thank you so much for your patience and encouragement.

To my bosses Joel and Stan, thanks for putting up with me for twenty years!

And lastly a special shout out to my beta readers: Jessi, Maureen, Tina, Darlene, and Patty... thank you for taking the time to read what I wrote and give me the honest feedback I desperately craved.

I set out to write the book I couldn't find when I was ten......I hope it is what you are looking for...

~Terri

For Tracy, our sweet angel in heaven....

Chapter 1

She had to get out of there! Marin grabbed a library pass from the study hall teacher and bolted up the two flights of stairs to her sanctuary.

This sucks! She thought as she slammed her books on the last open desk in the corner near the windows. Two older girls at a nearby table looked up from their studying and glared at her.

"Shush!" The librarian automatically said from her desk across the room, not bothering to stop sorting books.

Marin slipped into her seat and gave the girls an apologetic smile, not that she felt sorry. Marin closed her eyes and leaned her head against the cool brick wall as she struggled to keep the tears in.

Why would Chris choose Jenna over me? We've been lab partners all semester.... I thought we had something!

Marin took a peek at the kids at the adjacent tables and chairs. Mercifully no one was paying her any attention, so she put her head down on the desk, burying her face to let the tears win.

Marin stayed in this position for a few minutes. With a quick wipe of her eyes, she stole a glance out the window. The wind had picked up, making the tops of the trees sway. It looked like the daily afternoon thunderstorms might be rolling in early. She took a deep breath, closed her eyes, and willed herself to relax.

Soaring high above her house, Marin could see her whole neighborhood. Gently flapping her wings and veering to the left, she dropped lower and circled the house. She saw the blue paint that was starting to peel and the roof tiles that needed replacing. She could see her old swing set rusting in the backyard. She saw bicycles stored in the open shed behind her house.

The neighbor's dog began to bark at her as she dove lower, constantly searching. In a blink of her eye she caught movement; a field mouse out foraging. Claws extended, she used the air currents to propel herself forward toward her prey, reaching, screeching....

"Wow, look at that!"

Marin lifted her head and blinked, her neck stiff from sleeping on the desk. Her eyes dilated and glazed, she tried to focus on the culprits. The same girls who'd glared at her when she sat down were now pointing at the window where Marin was sitting. She gently shook her head in an effort to clear it, but that didn't work.

On the window ledge sat a Peregrine falcon intently watching her. Like a magnet to a piece of steel, Marin had to lean over to touch the window where it sat, tapping her fingers on the pane. In response, the falcon pecked where her hand was, then gently unfolded and refolded its wings. Annoyed, the bird began to pace back and forth, continuing to peck at the window.

The falcon definitely wanted in. And it's not afraid of me. Marin didn't know how she knew this, she just did.

Mesmerized by what they were seeing, the kids on her side of the room gathered around Marin's desk to watch. Anytime Marin placed her hand on the window, the falcon went over to it, unafraid and curious.

"Open it!" one boy coaxed.

"No, don't! Are you crazy?" another answered.

Marin slowly stood up and reached for the handle that would crank open the window. Just as the window opened wide enough to let it in, BZZZZZZZZZZ went the school bell that signaled the end of the class period. The falcon ruffled its feathers, opened its beautifully colored wings and leapt from the ledge.

Chapter 2

"What's wrong with you?" Amy asked, staring up at Marin. "Why aren't you answering me?" When Marin didn't answer again, she reached up to smack her lightly on the face and was rewarded when Marin finally focused on her. "Are you okay?"

"My neck hurts," she finally answered, reaching back to rub the sore spot.

"Come on, we gotta go." Amy demanded as she leaned Marin against the wall. "Take this," she added, giving Marin her bag. "I can't hold yours and mine."

Amy gripped Marin's arm and steered them toward the cafeteria.

"So, you gonna tell me what happened?"

"I fell asleep," Marin whispered.

"Again? That's the second time this week."

"Yeah, I can't help it. I haven't been sleeping at night," she added.

"You feeling better now? Should I take you to the nurse?"

"No, I'm good." Marin smiled, relaxing her grip on Amy as they continued to walk. "But something else happened today."

"Jill told me about Chris asking Jenna out. Sorry." Amy gripped Marin tighter in a little arm hug. She tried picking up the pace, but Marin continued to shuffle along.

"No, it's something else. I'll tell ya later," Marin said, her head finally beginning to clear while they walked.

"I assume we won't be trying to sit near Chris Avery again today?"

"Oh, we are. I've decided I'm not giving up that easy," Marin answered smiling at her best friend.

It would seem that with summer starting the following week, the whole Middle School was extra rambunctious. The sound from the cafeteria when they opened the door blasted them like a water hose in the face. There was singing from the choir in one corner, the drama kids were trying to stage an impromptu show in another, and the rest of the room was just... loud.

"Let's get our food and find Chris," Marin had to yell to Amy even though she was standing right next to her.

Ten minutes later, Amy and Marin were slowly walking down the main aisle searching for Chris, lunch trays in hand. They passed Marin's twin brother Josh and his best friend Danny sitting with members of her swim team. None of them looked up when the girls stopped in front of their table as they continued to scan the room.

"Where is he?" Marin yelled frustrated. "Did we miss him?"

With that, an apple went sailing past her face, just missing her.

"Oh crap," Amy exclaimed when she realized who threw it. Marin glanced to her left to see where it landed. She'd already seen who'd thrown it. It'd hit Sherri Lynn square in the forehead, the rotten pieces spewed onto the table all around her on impact. The poor thing looked dazed. Tears started to stream down her cheeks as she clutched her head.

Marin whirled to face the thrower, steam practically emanating off her with rage. "What the heck is wrong with you?"

"That's too bad, I wasn't aiming at her. I was aiming at the geek," he laughed, motioning to Bobby Lutz a few seats away from Sherri, turning his back on Marin.

"Don't turn your back on me, you jerk!" she screamed at him as she chucked the contents of her metal lunch tray toward his table, her sandwich and drink landing on the floor.

The fact that Peter Boyle was separated from her on the other side of his table didn't stop Marin. She picked up the now empty tray and in two seconds was standing on top of the table, towering over the bully. Instantly following her, Amy leapt up to stop Marin, grabbing her around her waist as she swung the tray with all of her might; the day's pent up frustration aimed at Peter Boyle's head.

Amy grabbing Marin pulled her off balance and she missed him by a mere inch. The swish of air past his head made Peter Boyle instinctively turn around and swing at Marin.

His hand connected with the metal tray, the sound of it crashing onto the floor echoed across the tile walls of the tiny cafeteria. Amy and Marin, their eyes wide with shock, stood gaping at the bully, the chilling silence washing over them like a wave.

Everyone in the cafeteria was staring at them. Amy and Marin immediately jumped down off the table to put some distance between them and the bully. The silence lasted only a few seconds and then a murmur in the back of the room began.

"Did you see that? He tried to hit a girl!"

The assistant principal Mr. Stack quietly appeared at Peter Boyle's side, flanked by the cafeteria monitor as they escorted him out of the room. The shade of red on Peter's face almost matched the shirt he was wearing.

Sherri was crying pitifully at this point. Their friends and a cafeteria aide helped her up and led her in the direction of the nurses' office. It looked like she already had a lump forming where the apple hit her.

"Are you okay?" Josh asked when he reached Marin's side.

Marin nodded. She bent down and started to toss her lunch back onto her tray but refused to look her brother in the face.

"What the heck were you thinking?"

"I was thinking that someone needed to hit him back," Marin replied evenly.

"You and your frigging temper." Josh stood glaring. "Did you think you could actually take on that guy?"

"Yep! Me and my tray!" Marin stood up and slammed the tray on the table for emphasis.

Josh recoiled, but he didn't say anything.

"Don't lecture me! He hurt Sherri! You know, it's not like I had time to think about it!"

"Obviously not!" Josh answered, frustration in his voice. "Marin, you're not getting my point. He swung at you and half the school saw it."

"Yeah, and I hope the jerk gets in extra trouble for that."

Looking Josh in the eyes she added, "I couldn't let him get away with it."

Josh gave her a pleading look. "Well, why does it have to be you?" Pausing a second, he continued, "Marin, what if Peter wants payback and you're alone?"

"School's almost out. I just have to be careful until vacation starts. Maybe he'll forget."

"Yeah, right. This isn't just about you now. This involves all of us, you, me and all of our friends."

"Do you really think he'd risk it? I mean come on, if something happens to me, who do you think they're gonna blame first?"

"Well, that's a consolation," Josh responded sarcastically.

Marin walked over to Josh and grabbed him by the arm. "You're not gonna tell Mom and Dad are you?"

"No way, crazy sister," he said shaking his head, giving up. "I want to go to the beach next Saturday. If you're grounded for fighting again, we both stay home," Josh added as he moved to walk back to his table with Danny.

Marin turned around to speak to Amy and tripped over Bobby Lutz. Bobby had come around the table too and was looking up at Marin with gratitude in his eyes. At four feet nine inches tall,

Bobby only came up to Marin's shoulder. "Thanks for standing up to him Marin," Bobby said with awe in his voice. Surprised, Marin looked down at him sheepishly. She had forgotten all about the bully's intended target. Flushing red, Marin was embarrassed that she hadn't even considered poor Bobby's feelings. "He almost always takes my lunch money or does something nasty to me," he added, his voice trailing off.

"What?" Marin responded astonished. "Why don't you tell someone and put a stop to it?"

"I'm afraid to. I'm afraid he'll really hurt me. He's promised to stuff me in a dumpster. Besides, it's my word against his. No one will stand up to him and say they saw him do it. You see how big he is. Haven't you heard the rumor he was left back?" Bobby questioned.

"Yeah, I have."

By this time, Bobby was literally wringing his hands with nervousness. Even though Mr. Stack had taken Peter Boyle to the principal's office, he was newly afraid of repercussions later. "I just give him my money every day." Bobby closed his eyes and shuddered.

Marin was even angrier now at Peter Boyle then she had been before. But she was at a loss as to what to do. Someone has to teach that bully a lesson and put a stop to him. At this point, Amy took a step closer to Marin and Bobby. Amy, who was the same height as Bobby, looked him directly in the eyes and shyly smiled at him. Bobby blushed and hastily turned to leave.

"Thanks again Marin," he said as he walked away from them toward the exit.

"Hey, no problem Bobby. Take care of yourself." She was utterly clueless as to how she could help him. Thoughts of seeing Chris Avery vanished from her mind.

Chapter 3

Approaching Danny at the bus stop later that day, Josh said, "My sister is crazy. What the heck is wrong with her trying to take on that jerk, Peter Boyle?"

"Only if she didn't dent that tray on his head," Danny added, smiling at the thought of Peter Boyle lying unconscious on the floor, knocked out by hundred and twenty pound Marin. "I don't think you realize how strong you guys are. You have swim practice, weight lifting, swim meets."

"Not to mention wrestling," Josh added slyly as he unsuccessfully tried to grab Danny in a head lock. Danny was too quick and wiry to let Josh get a good grip on him. Danny might not be a great swimmer, but he was on the baseball team. And he was strong too.

"Okay, you win this round," Josh said, his face getting all serious. Josh started pacing back and forth. "But what am I gonna do about Marin? Boyle took a swing at her. What if he goes after her again?"

"Nothing man. It's almost summer vacation. Maybe he'll forget about her?"

Josh shrugged. "That's what Marin said." Neither one of them spoke for a few minutes. "I don't know what we're gonna do," he said again as their bus pulled up.

****

That night after dinner, Marin had invited Amy over and they were camped out in Marin's room. "Just a few more days, and we'll officially be eighth graders," Amy said while looking at some photos on Marin's desk. "We will rule-the-school!"

"I know. I can't wait," Marin answered looking up from her from pile of notes.

"Hey, who's this Marin?" Amy asked holding up an old photo with two adults and two toddlers in it. "I don't remember seeing this before."

"Well," Marin answered, getting up off her bed and walking over to where Amy was sitting. "My mom found it when she started cleaning the attic last weekend. The little kid with the bright red hair is me and the one with the dark hair is Josh. Oh, and those are our birth parents," she added offhandedly pointing at the adults.

"Your birth parents? Wow. I thought that most adopted kids don't know who their birth parents are."

"Well, I thought I told you that we were adopted when we were around two years old or so? Our birth parents died in a boating accident and my mom and dad were the only family we had left. My mom and my birth mom are cousins or something like that," Marin replied gazing at the photo.

"Hmmm. I just thought you guys were adopted as babies," Amy answered, her voice trailing off.

"Nope. We were older. I don't really remember them. Did I mention that this was my birth parent's house?" she added while doing a slow turn with her arms up in the air. "Apparently it's been in the family for generations. So, not only did mom and dad get us kids when our birth parents died, they got this house too. I can just picture it. Here you go Mr. and Mrs. Royce. Not only do you get these kids, but they come with a bonus: a free house," Marin added with a giggle.

"You're crazy, Marin," Amy replied laughing.

"Did I also tell you that mom and dad used to live in New York before the accident? They decided it would be easier to move down here then to sell this house. I always wondered why they did that. I think it would be cool to live in New York."

"Nah, not me. Our family went to a wedding a couple of years ago in New York. New York gets cold! I couldn't believe how cold it was. I like the heat of Florida. We can go swimming almost all year round," Amy replied.

"I hope it's not too hot next week at Jacksonville Beach. We don't all get to go too often. Dad's business can get crazy. And then swim camp starting up next month. After that it's back to swim lessons and then school again before you know it," Marin added.

"I know I'm gonna miss you when you go to camp," Amy pouted.

"It's just for a few weeks, not too long. We'll still have some time left before school starts again," Marin replied with a little guilt in her voice.

"I wish I could go with you..."

"That would be so cool, but.... the last I recall; you don't swim very well."

"Thanks for reminding me. So, I guess you better give me another lesson when we go to the beach, huh Marin?" Amy asked looking up at her friend with her pretty almond-shaped eyes.

Marin smiled at Amy and shook her head. "Oh, alright.... we can try again if you want." Thoughts of their last disastrous swimming lesson went racing through Marin's head and she had to fight off the impulse to shudder. It's a bit embarrassing having a best friend who sinks every time she's in the water, Marin wanted to say, but didn't. "Okay, if you're game, I'm game. But, I need your help with something too. I have to figure out how to talk my Mom into changing the wallpaper in here. The more I sit in this room, the more it gets on my nerves. I can't stand it anymore."

"It's pretty gross," Amy agreed looking around at the large yellow flowers that covered the walls.

"I don't know where they got this nasty design, but it's ancient." Marin said reaching over and peeling off a small piece.

"Who knows?" Amy sat for a moment and thought. "I do have an idea for you though, now

22

that I think about it," she finally said. "It usually works for me when I want something."

"Awesome. Then we have a deal?"

"Deal."

****

Two days later Marin, Josh, Amy, and Danny were waiting at the bus stop after one of their final exams. They were excitedly talking when Peter Boyle approached the group and stood directly in front of Marin, staring at her, his hands clenched at his side. Uh, oh, Marin thought, this is it.

"You," he said pointing at her, "you're at the top on my list."

"Well, it sure beats being at the bottom of it," Marin replied calmly, looking up to meet his intense eyes. Josh quickly moved to his sister's side. Amy and Danny flanked them as well. Not that tiny Amy could do much, but Marin knew that wouldn't stop her from trying.

"What do you think you're doing threatening my sister, loud mouth?" Josh added with a gulp, standing up as straight as possible. Even though it was four against one, Peter Boyle was intimidating.

"She made me a laughingstock last week," Peter answered looking over the group of friends.

"You did that yourself," Marin replied, her pulse starting to race. As usual Marin's temper had started to flare. She couldn't back down from a fight if she felt threatened or if someone close to her was threatened. "You're lucky I didn't get a chance to teach you the lesson I wanted to," she taunted.

"And what lesson was that?" Peter countered, the rage on his face starting to look worse.

"The bigger they are, the harder they fall!" Josh answered for her.

"Yeah, you and what army?" Peter mocked, his eyes narrowing. He didn't seem to care that he was outnumbered, not one bit.

"Well, clearly I must have done something right, if you're standing here," Marin said, as a sly smile spread across her face.

"Just you wait. I'll get even," he growled, as their bus pulled up. Peter abruptly turned and started to walk away from them fast. The four of them watched his departure until he was completely out of their view. Marin stepped onto the bus followed by Josh, Amy, and Danny. Plopping herself down, Marin glanced out the window and saw the reason Peter had left so quickly. Mr. Stack was standing outside, facing the busses. She hadn't seen him before. He must have just gotten there.

Pointing out the window, Marin said, "Look, there's Mr. Stack. Peter Boyle is a chicken. Look how quickly he ran." The others agreed and laughed. Marin however, was just a little worried. She didn't want to think about another confrontation with that idiot. Josh was right. What if she was alone? Or what if it was Josh? This could get ugly real fast.

Chapter 4

The following week, Marin sent a text to Amy before she left her room and went downstairs to see if mom needed any help with dinner. "Finals are over! Beach tomorrow!" As she went to enter the kitchen, Marin stopped just outside the door. Her brother was standing across the room, arms folded, glaring at their Mom. "Why?" he asked with anger and frustration in his voice. "Why do I have to take my pill before we go the beach tomorrow?"

"You know why, Josh. Some social situations can be a little overwhelming for you because of your ADHD. The beach is going to be packed and loud. I just want you to be your focused best, and have a good time," Mom quickly added.

"But I won't have a problem Mom, I swear," Josh replied, crossing his heart. "It's not like school. It's just a trip to the beach. And you know that I sometimes get a headache from it. A headache would ruin my day..."

Shaking her head, Mom finally relented. "Alright Josh. Let's see how you handle yourself without it." Rushing over to her, Josh grabbed Mom in a quick hug. Looking up at the doorway, he noticed Marin and grinned at her.

"What's wrong with you?" Marin said, pretending she hadn't heard their conversation.

"Nothing," he answered, as he bounded out of the room and ran up the flight of stairs to his bedroom, whistling all the way.

"What's for dinner Mom? Is Dad gonna be home or does he have to work late?"

"I think he might be a little late tonight honey. I thought I'd make a salad, and we'd order a pizza for dinner. This way he can reheat it quick when he gets home."

"Dad sure works hard doesn't he?" Marin asked.

"He sure does. It's tough having your own business. Everything falls on the boss's head."

"Well, I'm sure glad you're a teacher Mom. Having summers off must be great. I know I love having you home with us," Marin said as she walked over to her mom and put her arms around her and gave her a kiss.

"Well, thanks honey," Mom said, enjoying the hug immensely.

"By the way, since you're in such a good mood, can we talk about the wallpaper in my room?"

"Okay," Mom looked at Marin, her eyebrows arching up slightly.

"Well," Marin continued, "Can we change it or paint it or do something with it? It's starting to drive me crazy."

"We'll see honey," Mom answered while grabbing a head of lettuce from the fridge for the salad.

Oh boy, that wasn't good, Marin thought. That usually meant they were headed for a "no" answer eventually. Marin let the subject drop as she started to help her mom with the salad.

"Um, Mom?" Marin asked a few minutes later, looking up from the tomato she was cutting. "Is it okay that I invited Jill and Amy to come with us to the beach tomorrow?"

"Sure honey. I told you guys you could each invite two friends."

"Great. Amy confirmed a yes, but I have to call Jill later and see if she can make it."

"I hope she can," Mom answered. "I feel so bad for her since her mom passed away last year. Oh, and thanks for reminding me. I need to call her dad and check in with him and see how he and Aaron are doing."

"Oh, well I have some news. Jill told me last week that Aaron has a new aide. He's an autism specialist from the school and he comes by to help out in the afternoons while Mr. Levy's at work. Jill said her dad really likes the job he's doing."

"That's great to hear. You want to call the pizza order in, or should I do it?"

"I'll do it!" Marin replied as she jumped up to grab the phone.

An hour later, Marin, Josh, and Mom were sitting at the dining room table enjoying their dinner when Dad arrived. He looked tired but happy. "Hi Dad," both kids chorused when he entered the room.

"I've got good news and some bad news. First the good news. I had a meeting with our accountant today and I think we might be able to afford a small vacation this year," Dad answered.

Both kids stopped mid-chew on their pizza when he said that and looked at him and Mom expectantly. "Mom and I will discuss options and money and let you guys know where we might be able to afford to go this year. You two can give us input of course," Dad said still smiling a big grin.

Marin and Josh were all smiles too. "I think we should go to Disney and maybe Universal Studios. Or, how about a trip to San Diego?" Marin asked.

"No, how about Nags Head or a camping trip or both?" Josh added bouncing up and down a little in his chair.

"Okay, thanks for the input guys," Mom said shaking her head. "Dad and I have to talk about this. We'll let you know."

"Hey Dad, can you still go to the beach with us tomorrow?" Josh asked.

"No, sorry, that's my bad news. I'm going to have to work. The new guy we hired didn't show up today, so I have to handle the store."

"It's okay Dad," Josh said as he got up to put his dish in the dishwasher. "We understand."

"We love you Dad," Marin said as she too got up. Then she went over and hugged her dad. "It doesn't matter where we go, as long as we get to go together."

"Wow. I should come home with good news all the time," Dad replied. "Hey Josh," Dad said as he turned to face his son who was rinsing his plate in the sink. "After I eat, are you up for a quick game of basketball? Marin, you want to play too?"

"How about we all play?" Mom added. "This ought to be fun!"

"Just don't get hurt this time Dad," Josh added laughing.

"Well, just promise to go easy on me okay?" Dad replied laughing, grabbing a scoop of salad to go with his pizza.

****

Later that night while Marin was getting ready for bed, she picked up the photo of her birth parents that Amy had commented on the week before. Try as she might, she couldn't remember them. She sat at the desk and held the photo up to her face so she could see it in the mirror and do a comparison. She decided that she looked a lot like her birth mother. Of course they shared the same red hair and freckles but she had her mother's nose as well. Josh looked exactly like their birth dad, with the dark hair and dark eyes.

Marin put the photo back on her desk. Turning off the bedroom light, she lay in the bed tossing and turning, excited about tomorrow's beach trip. I hope I don't dream again tonight, she thought as she finally drifted off.

Chapter 5

"Mom, you know I've been having the strangest dreams for the last couple of weeks," Marin said yawning as she entered the brightly lit kitchen the next morning.

"Well it happened again last night. Last night it was a cat, but a big cat like a lion. Last week I was swimming in the ocean like some kind of fish. And remember the falcon two weeks ago?"

"Well, you are a very good swimmer," Mom countered. "And we are going to the beach today. That might explain the fish dreams. I don't know about the cat or bird dreams," she said chuckling.

"Well, it's all so strange." Marin replied. "At least a lion wasn't here when I woke up," Marin added. "It's eerie. I'm actually seeing things as if I were the animal. The only bummer is that I'm so tired the next day. Oh, and I almost forgot to tell you," Marin continued, "Jill texted me this morning. She can't make it today. She's sick."

"Oh, no, that's too bad. I hope she feels better soon. Your brother invited Danny to join us,"

Mom added. "Have you seen Josh this morning, or is he still in bed on this beautiful day?"

"I guess he's still in bed. "Josh, are you up yet?" Marin walked over and screamed up the staircase. Without waiting for a reply she charged up the stairs stomping all the way, trying to make as much noise as possible. "Mom wants to know if you're awake," Marin yelled as she slammed the door to her bedroom, making the wall vibrate in the old house.

"I am now," Josh replied grumpily from behind his bedroom door.

"Get up you lazy slob! Extra sleep is not going to help you at the beach today! I'm still gonna kick your butt!" Marin said. "Hey Ma!" Marin yelled as she stuck her head out of her room. "Should I bring my camera? I'll be careful with it."

Marin decided to bring the camera anyway, even if mom objected. She wanted to record her victory for the whole world to see. Gee, I can't wait to race Josh again, she thought. It's so much fun to beat him.

Oh boy, I gotta make sure I put on tons of sunscreen today. These freckles are getting out of hand. They are everywhere, she thought as she inspected her arms and hands. There are so many it almost looks like a tan. At least my blue eyes pop out more. That's the only consolation.

"Hey nerd," Josh called out. "I hope you're ready to lose today!"

"You wish," Marin replied from her room as she got dressed.

"Hey, none of that you two," mom yelled from the kitchen. "Both of you get your bathing suits on and come and have breakfast. Then we can pack lunches and get ready to pick up your friends. Josh, is Danny still coming with us?"

"Yeah mom. I spoke to him yesterday," Josh replied as he entered the kitchen.

"Good, we'll pick him up first, and then we'll pick up Amy on our way to the highway."

Sitting in the car an hour later, Marin and Josh were excitedly talking to their friends and ignoring each other. Danny and Josh were playing their handheld video games while Marin was showing Amy the basic operation of her digital camera. "I want you to take pictures and video of our race Amy," Marin whispered. "This way I can post it online for the whole world to see."

"Do you think that's a good idea? What if you lose?" Amy asked under her breath, trying to keep her voice as low as possible.

"Thanks a lot Amy. Way to be supportive of your best friend," Marin replied.

"You know I'm on your side, but?" Amy countered. "Josh is a little bigger than you."

"Yeah, I know, but not by much, and I'm faster," Marin answered defensively.

"I just want to be really tall, or at least as tall as Josh gets. That way I can keep beating him."

"You already swim fast," Mom interjected, eavesdropping on their conversation. "You're both on the swim team. You've both won medals and trophies. What more do you need?"

"I don't know. I just want to keep on winning," Marin answered ruefully.

"Well, if you continue to practice, I'm sure you will. Just don't forget that swimming isn't everything. I know you're only thirteen years old, but college and a career should be in your future as well," Mom said.

"Aw, Ma not again," Josh piped in, trying to head off a lecture.

"Hey I know, maybe I'll be a swim coach!" Marin answered. Amy couldn't stop herself and burst out laughing.

"Well, we'll see." Mom chuckled too, as she pulled the minivan into the beach parking lot.

"Okay gang. We're here. Josh, you and Danny grab the coolers. Marin and Amy grab the chairs. I'll take the umbrella and bags."

"I so love the ocean," Marin exclaimed as they all scrambled to collect their stuff from the vehicle. "Pools are okay, but the ocean is alive. It moves and twists and turns and can toss you like a rag doll when you least expect it."

"Perfectly said," Mom answered. "And don't forget to never turn your back on it."

"Ma," Josh whined. "You've told us this like a hundred times already."

"Well, I'm telling you again," Mom answered. "All of you please be careful. Stay within the boundaries of the lifeguards. And NO racing!"

After emptying the vehicle of its contents, the five of them made their way through the crowds looking for a place to plop down their stuff. Finally after what seemed like an eternity of walking on the hot sand, they found a spot and started setting up the umbrella and blankets. Mom pulled Marin and Josh aside. "Okay you two. I mean it. No racing today. This beach is packed. I don't want anyone doing anything stupid, or I swear this will be the last time we come here," Mom warned. Marin and Josh glanced at each other and slightly rolled their eyes, but neither one replied. "Okay, both of you?" Mom asked. Both Josh and Marin nodded. Josh turned away and Mom grabbed Marin and pulled her aside. "Marin please don't bait Josh. You know what having ADHD does to him. He is impulsive enough as it is. I don't need you to instigate," Mom pleaded.

"I said okay Mom," Marin answered dejectedly. She had really been looking forward to racing Josh today.

"Okay, have fun everyone!" Mom yelled to the group. And with that, all of the kids made a beeline for the water.

"Wow, is this great!" Amy exclaimed splashing around in knee deep water as she watched Marin dive into the first approaching wave. The boys did the same thing, but a little further away, pretending they weren't with them.

After lunch, Amy and Marin walked along the shore taking photos with Marin's camera while Marin gave her pointers. Pointing the camera at the water, Amy zoomed in with the lens. To their right about fifty feet away from the shore was a group of kids having a splash fight. Looking away from the camera, Amy squinted from the glare, straining to see them. "Hey, Marin! You see those guys out there with Danny and Josh?" she said, pointing them out. "I think they go to our school."

"Oh wow, they sure do. And hey, is that Chris Avery?" Marin stammered a bit, a slight blush spreading on her cheeks.

"Sure looks like it!" Amy answered as she squinted again in their direction, shielding her eyes with her hand.

"Wow you've got good eyes Amy! Use the camera and zoom in on them! Is it him? Is Jenna with him?"

"It's him." Amy did as she was told. "And Jenna's not there."

"Let's see if we can casually make our way over to them," Marin giggled. Amy took one step into the water and Marin grabbed her arm and stopped her. "Amy," Marin exclaimed. "You can't go in the water holding my camera. Besides, I need you to stay here and record this. I'm getting a bad feeling. I think I see Sean Thomas with them."

As Marin made her way to them, she could see that one of the boys was indeed Chris Avery. And with him was Angelo Libretti and Sean Thomas-the same Sean Thomas who's on the swim team with Josh. Uh oh, Marin thought. This isn't good. Those two are constantly trying to best each other. They are worse than me and Josh.

Even though the water was warm, Marin got a cold chill down her spine. The boys had stopped splashing. She could barely make out what Sean Thomas was saying, but she didn't really need to. He was pointing at a buoy that was about 50 yards away- and way out of bounds for the lifeguards.

"Josh is a chicken, Josh is a chicken...cluck, cluck, cluck." Marin could now hear as she approached them. Oh crap! Marin thought. Mom is gonna be so ticked off. Marin glanced toward the shore and saw Amy holding her camera. Oh, I hope she gets all this, Marin thought as she waved to Amy. I don't want to be the one who gets in trouble for this.

Mere seconds later, Chris called out, "on your mark, get set, go!" Sean and Josh executed a standing dive into the waist deep water and began swimming toward the buoy, almost as if they were being chased by a shark. Uninvited, Marin joined the race and quickly caught up to them.

None of them stopped when the shrill call of the lifeguard's whistle, immediately followed by an air horn sounded as they breeched the lifeguard boundary. All three kept going, their goal mere seconds away now. Moments later and breathing hard, Marin stretched out her hand to grab the buoy and claim her victory, Sean barely a second behind her.

Hanging on to the buoy to catch her breath, Marin looked back toward the beach to see where her brother was. Fear and panic rose inside her as she scanned the sea. Josh wasn't in her view. "Where's Josh?" she breathlessly yelled to Sean. "I don't see him!"

"Over there!" Sean pointed to their left. Josh wasn't behind them, but parallel to them, doing his best to tread water.

Marin could make out Josh's head bobbing up and down with the waves. "Josh!" she screamed. "Josh!"

"Help!" He yelled back. "It won't let me go-riptide! Get some help! I can't fight it. I'm cramping!" Josh started to wave his hands frantically at this point, sheer panic overriding everything he knew about riptides.

"Hold on," she yelled back. "I'm coming!" Marin released her grip on the buoy, just as Sean grabbed her arm to stop her.

"Riptide Marin!" he warned, clearly still out of breath and breathing hard. "It'll get you too!"

"Let go of me! I can't leave him! I have to!" Marin screamed in a rage of fear, yanking her arm away from him. Glancing toward the shore, she watched as the life guards scrambled into their rescue raft. Panic set in as she began a frantic breathless swim to reach her brother; they wouldn't get there in time to save him.

"No, don't fight it Josh. Swim with it, not against it! Float!" She tried shouting to him between strokes, trying to calm him. But it did no good. Josh was attempting to swim against the tide that was trying to push him out to sea, and getting weaker by the second with the futile effort.

Oh boy do I wish I was a dolphin now, Marin thought seconds later she watched with horror as Josh lost his battle with the ocean and went under. No, I'm so close! Using every last ounce of her strength, Marin picked up her pace, took a deep breath and dove under the water reaching for her brother.

Amy was still watching and recording from the shore when she saw what was happening to Josh. She ran yelling and screaming to the nearest lifeguard tower, which had already mobilized to help. They were on alert and could clearly see someone was in distress now.

As soon as Marin took off after Josh, Sean started yelling for the lifeguards and waving his hands, all while desperately holding on. Meanwhile, he was panicked too, because not only did Josh go under and not come up, he saw Marin do the same thing.

Seconds later, a spray of water plumed into the air, immediately followed by a long sleek nose and dorsal fin breaking the surface. With a small splash, Josh was bobbing up and down on the waves coughing and gasping. Josh gripped the creature tightly by two of its fins as it started to swim powerfully toward the shore and the approaching lifeguards. When the dolphin was within reach of the boat, Josh released his grip and it propelled him toward the lifeguards, who hauled him in. The lifeguards then helped Josh continue to expel the water he'd swallowed. Pausing to watch this, the dolphin silently turned and disappeared beneath the foamy water.

The lifeguards then maneuvered their boat to retrieve Sean. "Where's Marin?" he yelled as they reached down and pulled him in the boat. "She went down at the same spot!" he added, pointing to the place he last saw her.

"Marin's missing?" Josh choked. "She was so close to me, so close," his voice trailed off, his dazed eyes now scanning the empty sea.

Turning their dingy back to look for her, both lifeguards took turns diving in the area, but came up empty handed. They radioed in to the Coast Guard for extra help.

Mom and Amy were crying. At first, they saw the fin and started to panic. A shark! But no, they saw with relief that it was a dolphin. Mom could see Josh and Sean in the boat, but couldn't tell from the beach if they had Marin too. Panic began to well inside Mom when she saw the boat reach the buoy, but didn't see Marin anywhere. "Amy," Mom cried, "do you see Marin in that boat?"

"No," Amy squeaked fearfully. "I don't see her anywhere."

"Where's Marin?" Mom screamed to the lifeguards, but they couldn't hear her.

The lifeguards dropped the boys at the shore. An emergency crew placed an oxygen mask on Josh and wrapped him in a light blanket to help with the shock. "Mom, I'm so sorry, so sorry," Josh said, choking on tears. Mom leaned over and embraced Josh in a hug. Collapsing next to him in the sand, she continued to scan the ocean for her daughter, her swollen eyes almost useless.

The lifeguards closed the beach to swimming and rallied the Coast Guard to look for Marin. Word went out on the beach, and soon everyone capable of searching was enlisted to help. Boats and helicopters assembled and started a sweep of the area. They found a small pod of three dolphins frolicking a half mile off shore, but no Marin.

Mom called Dad, and he too was now at the beach. "There were hundreds of people here today. How can one little girl disappear?" Dad asked to no one in particular.

Danny, Chris, Angelo, Sean, and Amy huddled together sitting on blankets next to Josh. "Maybe she was swept out to sea," Angelo whispered.

"She's a strong swimmer, she could be okay," Amy added.

"I didn't see her come up," Sean countered with a pained expression on his face. "I saw her dive down, but..." his voice trailing off.

"I still can't believe a dolphin pulled you up Josh," Chris said in awe.

"Where did it come from?" Danny asked.

"Did everyone see it?" Josh asked looking around at the group.

"We all saw it," Amy replied gazing at the water. "We could see it from the beach." The boys all nodded in agreement.

By now, the local television news station had arrived with their cameras and news reporters. The local newspaper was there as well. Reports of a dolphin saving a boy from drowning and his missing twin sister disappearing were big news. The news crews did their best to interview anyone who would talk. All of Josh's and Marin's friends were asked what they saw, and what they thought had happened. The lifeguards were all interviewed as well. Everyone agreed on one thing. A dolphin did indeed bring up Josh and propel him toward the lifeguards in the boat.

Two hours of exhaustive searching went by. A small crowd of volunteers assembled and set up a tent, offering food and drink to the searchers. Amy and Danny's parents arrived to take them home but none of the kids wanted to go, not without word of Marin.

Suddenly, a cry came out from the walkie-talkie. They'd found her! More importantly, she was alive! Marin was brought back to the tent on a small all-terrain vehicle belonging to the lifeguards. They'd found her almost two miles away walking haphazardly on the shore line. She'd been stumbling and staggering as she tried to walk. At first glance they thought she was drunk and almost overlooked her. But then they noticed how young she was and questioned her. Marin told them that she was there with her mother and brother and their friends, but she couldn't find them.

Marin's hair was matted with seaweed and her suit was torn in a few places. She was so completely drained of energy that one of the lifeguards had to help her walk. "I don't know what happened," Marin whispered to her parents, collapsing into her father's arms. "One-minute I was trying to save Josh, and the next I'm on the beach way on the other side of the jetty," she added pointing over her shoulder, still gripping her dad tightly.

Josh was so happy to see her; he grabbed her out of his father's arms and squeezed with all of his might. "Oww. You're hurting me," Marin said. Turning to the look at the others, she saw Chris Avery staring and smiling at her. Blushing, she pushed Josh away and fell face first into the sand.

"Marin, are you okay?" Amy asked, as she and Josh helped her up. "I feel beat up, but okay," Marin answered with a weak smile, brushing sand off. Dad took over at this point, supporting her under her arms so she wouldn't fall again.

The news crews went crazy. Camera flashes started going off and microphones were shoved in Marin and Josh's faces. Everyone wanted to hug Marin and see how she was. And of course, all of the news people wanted an interview. Thanking the Coast Guard, the lifeguards, and all of the volunteers, Mom and Dad did their best to get Marin and Josh out of there as quickly as possible.

Once Mom and Dad had Josh and Marin in the car alone, boy did they hear it. Josh felt they deserved it. They had raced after all, and against the strict orders of Mom not to do so. Marin was so physically spent that she fell asleep in the minivan while the tirade was going on.

She was still so tired that when they got home, Mom and Dad each put an arm around her to help her up the stairs to her room. Marin was asleep before Mom could finish helping her into her pajamas.

Chapter 6

That night Marin woke with a start. She'd been dreaming again. But instead of dreaming about being some kind of animal, this time it was replay of what had happened at the beach. Sitting upright in her bed, Marin struggled to recall the day's events. She had been racing with the guys, but Josh got caught in a riptide. She tried to help him. She saw him go under and she dove underwater to rescue him. Then what? She couldn't remember the next two hours until after she was found by the lifeguards. How can that be?

What else am I missing? Marin lay there thinking. Finally, she decided she couldn't take it anymore and went to the bathroom to take a shower. She needed it. She stunk of seawater, salt, and suntan lotion.

Think, Marin, think, what else happened? There has to be something else. Suddenly a cold chill went up her spine as a realization struck her. She'd been thinking about a dolphin the instant before she dove down to save Josh.

What am I, some kind of dolphin whisperer? Or maybe I can communicate telepathically with them? Marin thought to herself laughing. But how did a dolphin show up just at the point that I wished for it?

This is crazy, she thought turning the water off in the shower. Climbing into clean pajamas, Marin went back to her room and bed. I'm gonna have to talk to Amy and the boys tomorrow about this. Someone had to have seen something else.

Josh woke up that night when he heard the shower running. He'd been having a weird dream too. In his dream, the dolphin that had saved him had blue eyes. Can a dolphin have blue eyes? I must have been seeing things. I'm going to have to look that up tomorrow online and see what I can find. He sleepily rolled over and closed his eyes again in an effort to go back to sleep.

****

Even though both kids managed to fall back to sleep after all they'd been through, Marin tossed and turned for the rest of the night in a fitful sleep. Waking up, she still felt drained. But she knew she needed to see if she could get some answers.

Someone had to have seen something else yesterday.

Marin got out of bed and turned on her cell phone. It started chiming instantly. She easily had over a hundred text messages and numerous voice mail messages. Wow, she thought. Scrolling through the messages she came upon a few phone numbers she didn't recognize. One caught her eye and she beamed when she read it. It was from Chris Avery. He texted her that he had gotten her number from a friend of hers. He wanted to know if she was okay. She couldn't think about him right now though. She was on a mission.

"Can you come over today? We need to talk," she texted to Amy.

"How are you feeling?" Amy quickly replied.

"Okay, but we gotta talk privately," Marin texted back. Marin was hoping against hope that maybe Amy had some answers. In the meantime, Marin could hear Josh in the bathroom. Quietly, so Mom and Dad couldn't hear her, she knocked lightly on the bathroom door.

"Josh, can we talk?" Marin whispered.

"Okay, give me a minute," Josh answered.

Quietly closing the bathroom door, Josh went to see Marin in her room. He was still limping a little. He stood at the entrance to her room straining to hear where mom was in the house. After a moment, he heard her rattling around in the kitchen. "What's going on? Why all the secrecy?"

"Ssshhh, I don't want mom to hear us," Marin answered. "I need to ask you a few things about yesterday."

"Okay, like what?" Josh replied. He wasn't really in the mood to go over the events of yesterday. He felt guilty enough as it was that they both could have died out there.

"I want to know exactly what you saw from the beginning of the race all the way to the time that you were brought back to shore," Marin asked.

"Well," Josh started, "there isn't much to say. I thought I was racing with Sean to the buoy. You arrived and joined us. I would have beaten him, but I got a cramp in my leg and then the riptide grabbed me. I panicked and went under," he continued while looking down at his leg remembering.

"What about the dolphin," Marin added. "What happened with that?"

"I don't know. Like I said, I panicked. I went under instead of trying to tread water...the pain in my leg was awful. It's still sore."

"You don't remember seeing the dolphin before you went under?" Marin asked.

"No, not at all. I only saw you and Sean at the buoy," Josh quickly added. "But I think I did see something strange. It woke me up last night and I can't get the picture of it out of my head."

"What?" Marin asked intrigued.

"I think the dolphin that saved me had blue eyes," Josh said looking up to gaze directly into his sisters eyes.

"Wait, what?" Marin replied. Her mouth was hanging open at this point in the conversation. "Can a dolphin have blue eyes? We've been to the aquarium a bunch of times. Have you ever seen a dolphin like that before?"

"No, but let's see if we can look it up online," Josh quickly added

Marin flipped open her laptop and tried searching for information on dolphins. While she found out all kinds of photos of them, none had blue eyes. They all had small black eyes. And Josh confirmed the type of dolphin that had rescued him. It appeared to have been a bottlenose dolphin.

Both kids were beyond confused at this point when Marin suddenly remembered her camera. "Let's see what Amy got with this," she said holding up her camera. They sat at Marin's desk while Marin went through her camera's controls to see what Amy caught with it. Toggling through the still photos, Marin saw the usual beach things: seashells, seagulls, and people all over the place in the water and on the shore. Nothing very helpful at first popped out at them until she came to the pictures of the race.

"Here we go," Marin said aloud. She saw photos of Chris, Angelo, and Sean before the race. Then photos of the boys after Josh and Danny reached them. And finally she came to the race photos of herself, Sean, and Josh. At that point the still photos ended, and Amy must have switched to video. Marin grabbed her cord for the camera and plugged it into her laptop. She wanted to be able to see as many details as she could.

Playing back the video, they could hear all kinds of yelling going on in the background. Next the piercing whistle of the lifeguard as Marin watched the three of them breach the lifeguard boundary. They saw Marin reach the buoy first, and then swim toward Josh. No sign of a dolphin anywhere.

Both Marin and Josh were holding their breath while they watched this. They were up to the part where Josh had gone underwater and Marin dove under to save him. And then up he came, holding onto the dolphin. It was actually very exciting to watch, Marin reflected. Both kids could see the lifeguards reaching Josh and then Sean. Amy had zoomed in to the maximum that the camera would allow, but it wasn't enough. They couldn't see the color of the dolphin's eyes. "Must have been some kind of genetic freak," Josh mused.

"Okay, that's it," Marin said. "We're going to need to talk to Danny and Amy. Maybe they saw something. I sent Amy a text this morning. I don't know what good it may do though. Even if one of them did see the dolphin better, what does it having blue eyes even mean?" Marin questioned.

Amy arrived an hour later. Mom had reluctantly agreed to let her come over. She was still very upset with both kids. And it didn't help that Marin and Josh had been all over the news yesterday complete with photos splashed across the front page of the local newspaper that morning.

Neither of her parents had decided yet if they were going to be grounded or to what extent. Marin and Josh both expected to be though, so the fact that Amy was allowed over was a bonus. Neither one of them did their usual morning teasing at breakfast. Both of them got up and cleared the table. Josh did the dishes. Marin went downstairs to the basement and started a load of laundry while Mom went to run some errands. Both of them decided it was wise to be on their best behavior.

"So, what's going on?" Amy asked as she entered the kitchen. "You guys look tired. How are you both feeling?" Amy had a way of getting right to the point. She also had a habit of being extremely blunt. Honest, but blunt. Marin liked to go clothes shopping with her for that very reason. Whatever you do, don't ask Amy a question if you don't want an honest answer.

"Marin and I want to know if you saw anything funny or strange yesterday regarding the dolphin," Josh asked. "We've gone over the photos and video you took and wanted to know if you could add anything else."

"Like what?" Amy replied, her interest now piqued.

Marin and Josh both looked back and forth at each other trying to decide how to phrase what they wanted to ask her. Marin jumped in first. "Amy, how well did you see the dolphin? More specifically, did you see the color of its eyes?"

"The color of its eyes?" Amy repeated, pausing before continuing. "I didn't see its eyes, not really."

"Crap," Josh and Marin both answered at the same time. "We were hoping you had," Marin added. "It's all very strange Amy. Here look at the video," Marin said while she pushed the keys on her laptop.

"I'm not sure what to think at this point. I dove under wishing I was a dolphin and then one suddenly appeared. What does that mean?" Marin continued.

Amy, who had been seated next to Marin to watch the video, stood up at this point and began pacing around the room. "It means nothing Marin," Amy answered with a furrowed brow. "I just think it's a coincidence." Josh and Marin both looked at her expectantly.

"I mean, what else could it be? What logical explanation can there possibly be for this?" Amy considered.

While they sat in silence contemplating, Marin and Josh heard their mom's minivan pull into the driveway. All three kids went outside to greet her and see if she needed any help bringing in her purchases. Mom had gone to the local paint and hardware store to pick up some supplies. Apparently Marin had gotten her wish to have her room redone. The only problem for Marin and Josh was that they were going to be doing most of the work as part of their punishment.

Marin's room had a few layers of wallpaper on it that needed to be scraped off before any painting or renovation could be done. Marin and Josh were going to spend the next two weeks doing just that. Amy made a hasty departure after they brought in all of the supplies. She wanted to help out, but she had a dentist appointment to go to. Mom said that she and Dad would help out too, as much as they could. That led Mom to her second announcement that morning.

Mom decided to do some tutoring during the summer. Both she and Dad thought it couldn't hurt to have the extra money even though Dad's business had picked up. She was going to start next week and that meant they would be alone during the day for the next few weeks before swim camp started.

Marin and Josh agreed that they would do their best to get along. Besides, they now had work to do to keep them occupied. They weren't going to be grounded exactly, but they weren't allowed to have friends over when no adults were home. And mom also gave them another project to work on, cleaning out the attic. Oh boy, Josh thought. This isn't grounding, it's free labor. Mom wants us to get along and do work together? Geez.

Mom's third announcement was the vacation destination. They would rent a small motor home and go camping. Josh suspected Mom and Dad would suspend or even cancel their camping trip if the kids screwed up again, so this was their incentive to behave and work together.

Marin and Josh got to work. They set up two tarps to cover Marin's furniture. Then each took a section of the room and started scraping. This was slow and tedious work. Scraping one layer wouldn't have been so bad, but they had to deal with three layers. After about an hour, they hadn't gotten very far when Mom called upstairs. Jill was here. "Oh crap," Marin said. "I totally forgot I invited her over today. I guess she's feeling better."

"Did your Dad drop you off Jill?" Mom asked as she led Jill into the kitchen.

"Yes. He said he'd be back at 3 pm to pick me up if that's okay?"

"Sure, honey. Marin and Josh are about to eat lunch now. You can join them. I've got to go out for a little bit."

"Hi Jill!" Marin said hugging her friend. "Um...we have work to do in my room after lunch. You wanna help?"

"Sure. Anything."

After they heard Mom close the front door on her way out, Marin looked up from her sandwich. Jill was sitting across the table from them staring at Josh, her blue eyes unblinking...just staring. They had been eating in silence and now Marin knew the reason why. Jill was shy and timid around boys, even ones she knew like Josh. But this was extreme, Marin thought.

"So," Marin said loudly making both Jill and Josh jump in their seats. "You wanna know about what happened yesterday?"

"I've been waiting for you guys to tell me," she answered quietly.

After Josh and Marin took turns telling Jill their story of their beach outing, the three of them reluctantly got busy scraping. Marin was secretly pleased that Jill agreed to help them with her room. She didn't have to after all. It wasn't her punishment. But Marin was happy none the less. Jill is such a sweetie. Or maybe she was helping out so she could spend time with Josh too, Marin thought.

Josh and Marin pushed her dresser from the corner wall so they could get at the wallpaper there.

Jill staked out a spot to start scraping near Marin, but with a view of Josh, Marin noticed with a grin.

Marin put on some music to help ease the boredom and tediousness of their work. Yep, Marin thought. Jill must have a crush on Josh. That's the third time in the last five minutes that I've caught her glancing at him.

They'd been at it for about twenty minutes when Jill gasped. None of the kids had been too talkative at that point, so it stopped them in their tracks. At first Marin thought that Jill had must have hurt herself. The scrapers have a sharp edge and you have to be very careful when you use them. Mom had gotten them gloves but you could still do damage if you weren't careful.

"Marin," Jill said, "Look at this." Jill had uncovered a small drawer in the wall that had been covered up with wallpaper. The drawer was maybe eight inches wide by three or so inches deep. Marin bent down to try to open it, using her fingers to pry it open, but she couldn't budge it. Josh tried as well, but he couldn't open it either. The glue from the wallpaper had done an excellent job of sealing it.

"I know what we need," Josh said as he quickly left the room. Two minutes later he was back with a screwdriver and a hammer. Josh inserted the screwdriver into the narrow opening and hit it lightly with the hammer. The drawer moved a bit. Tapping it again on the other side, Josh got the drawer to move again. Josh continued to tap all around the edges of the drawer to loosen the glue. Five minutes of this and Josh succeeded in getting the drawer open. Inside they discovered a small brown leather diary. Or at least that is what it looked like at first.

All three of them sat on the floor with Josh in the middle, holding the book on his lap. On the outside of it engraved in gold, was a giant letter P. Inside they found a chronological list of names. Next to the names were details of the people; places of birth, dates of birth, and dates of death. They only figured out what they were reading when they got to the last entries. The last entries were the names of Josh and Marin's birth parents; only the entries for their dates of death were missing.

Josh and Marin were actually speechless. Neither of them knew what to make of this list of names. Jill broke the silence first. "So, who are these people Marin," she asked tapping the book.

Josh answered her. "It looks like some kind of family tree. Our birth parents are the ones listed last," he said as he pointed them out to her. "This must have been placed in that drawer before we were born. We're not on it."

"Wow. That's way cool," Jill said as she stood up and brushed small pieces of wallpaper off her shorts. "Well, I gotta go."

"I'll walk you out Jill," Marin said as they headed downstairs.

When they got to the front door, Jill gave Marin a quick hug. "See ya."

"Take care, Jill. You know you can call or text anytime you need to talk," Marin said with a smile.

Jill smiled back warmly at her then turned and left the house. Hmmm, Marin thought. I've never seen her so quiet. She's usually so chatty when she comes over to see me. It must be Josh.

Marin went back upstairs to look at the book again and talk to Josh about it. There were so many names in that book. Some of them looked to be authentic Scottish and Irish names and the dates went back over three hundred years. Both kids couldn't wait to show it to Mom and Dad.

Dad actually made it home early that night. Dinner was spaghetti and meatballs, Marin's favorite. "Hey Mom, Dad," Josh said as soon as they sat down to eat. "Look what Marin and I found today in her room," Josh added as he put the book on the table. "Actually, Jill found it. It was in a secret drawer in the corner of her room, covered up by the wallpaper. I had to pry the door open to get it out."

Mom and Dad looked expectantly at the book. Dad opened it and started reading aloud. "Dugald married Annabella, Aiden married Mai, Maeve married Barry, Allana married Tierney, wow. So many Irish and Scottish names are here Caitlyn," he said while glancing at his wife and thumbing through the book. "This looks like a listing of our family tree, but why there is a giant P on the cover, who knows."

"And you guys found this in Marin's room?" Mom asked. "I can't see why it would be in a drawer hidden away. This is important family information."

"Maybe they forgot it was in there when they repapered my room," Marin answered.

"Looks like it's one of those mysteries we may never know the answer to," Dad supplied. Marin and Josh glanced at each other when he said that.

Another mystery, Josh thought. This is getting to be an interesting summer.

Chapter 7

Marin and Josh spent the whole next week and a half scraping the wallpaper off in Marin's room. Once all the wallpaper was off, the kids threw a painting party. Danny, Amy, and Jill were invited over and everyone got to work painting Marin's room. It didn't take them very long to finish up, especially with Mom and Dad supervising. After they were done, Mom and Dad cranked up the barbeque so they could all relax. Josh and Marin were pleased that they got to see their friends even though it meant they all had to work. It had been a fun day though.

Marin and Josh got up the next day knowing that they would have to start cleaning out the attic. They were to form piles of things to give away, things to keep, and things to sell at a yard sale. Some of the stuff Mom and Dad had already gone through and it was just a matter of bringing it down from the attic.

Marin and Josh got busy working right after breakfast. Old houses don't come with air conditioning in the attic, so they set up fans to help with the heat. Summers in northern Florida got hot. But it was no use. It didn't take long for the sweat to start running down their backs. Thankfully they were only required to work for a couple of hours a day because of the heat.

They hadn't been working very long when they heard the doorbell ring. Josh ran downstairs to get it while Marin continued to look through boxes. Straining, Marin could hear voices. A moment later, two heads peeked around the corner as they climbed the stairs and entered the attic. Danny had come over to see Josh.

Marin wasn't happy. Josh was breaking the rules and they could lose out on their camping trip. Marin stopped what she was doing and stood up still holding a small lamp, her eyes trying to bore a hole through Josh. He knew darn well that they weren't allowed to have friends over when mom and dad weren't home.

"Hi Danny," Marin mumbled between clenched teeth.

Josh stiffened and stopped at the entranceway. Marin looked like a tea pot about to boil over. Her ears and face were bright red, almost matching her hair.

"Josh, are you out of your mind? Aren't we still in trouble around here? I thought you wanted to go camping?"

"I do," Josh answered evenly. He was doing his best not to rile up his sister any more than he could, but darn it, he wanted to see his friend. Danny stood next to Josh and did not utter one word. He knew better.

"So, if you want to go camping, why is Danny here?" she asked pointing at him.

"Because, I wanted to see him. Mom and Dad won't find out unless you tell them," he taunted. "Who's gonna tell them?"

"What do you think I am, stupid? Of course I won't tell them, but what about someone else, like a neighbor or Danny's parents? Did that occur to you?" she asked, the volume of her voice rising. Marin was so enraged, she could practically see red.

"What you need is something to bite you in your butt! Then maybe you'd listen," Marin yelled. Using all of her might, she threw the lamp, shattering it. It left a gaping hole in the ancient attic wall.

Josh and Danny stopped breathing. In the instant that Marin threw the lamp, she collapsed onto the floor, landing on her hands and knees. Her body started to shake and her head hung facing down. Moments later her back arched up like a cat, and she looked up at Josh and Danny with the face of a German Shepherd. The rest of her body trembled uncontrollably as fur sprouted, rippling out from the middle of her back, replacing her skin and clothes. Less than ten seconds after uttering those words to Josh, a large German Shepherd dog now stood where Marin had been. It looked at them with big blue eyes, lowered its head and growled.

Josh and Danny sprang from the attic, slamming the door behind them as Marin the dog attacked the door.

"Holy crap! Did you see that?" Danny exclaimed. "I can't believe it!" both boys stood against the door holding it closed while Marin the dog clawed and barked trying to get at them.

"Marin," Josh said softly. "Marin, calm down. Can you hear me?"

"Marin, it's us." Danny joined in trying to calm her as well.

A couple of minutes passed while the boys spoke softly to her. Eventually the growling and clawing subsided. They stood at the door with their ears pressed against it but they couldn't hear anything. A few more minutes passed.

Josh said, "Marin, it's me Josh. We're coming in. Don't hurt us."

"Are you sure you should open the door?" Danny asked his eyes pleading with Josh. "She just tried to bite us."

"You don't have to go in. I'll go." Josh quietly opened the attic door and peeked inside. He didn't see her, so he bravely re-entered the attic to see what she was doing and if she was okay. Reluctantly, Danny followed behind him, stepping quietly.

Marin the dog was busy sniffing the hole in the wall where the lamp had damaged it. Marin looked up at the boys as they approached her and whined, her tail slowly wagging. Josh reached out to her and she sniffed his hand in a friendly greeting.

"Guess I know how a dolphin saved me last month," Josh said to Danny while staring at Marin. Danny still looked a little afraid of the dog but that changed after Josh's statement.

Neither boy knew what was going to happen next. Marin's rage had gone, but how long would she remain in the form of a dog? Josh had no clue what if anything he and Danny should be doing. The only thing they both agreed on was that they had to keep an eye out for Marin and definitely not let her out of the house.

"Do you know anything about dogs?" Josh questioned.

"I really hope she's housebroken," he added and shook his head in amazement.

"And what about fleas?" Danny questioned with a grin on his face, joining in the fun.

They both laughed aloud at that. "Marin doesn't have fleas!" he exclaimed still chuckling. "If she didn't have them before, she won't have them now!"

"Then I guess she'll be housebroken too!"

The tension in the room had been so thick you could cut it with a knife. But the simple and silly act of comparing Marin with a real dog had broken it. Both boys felt a bit better after that. And since neither Josh nor Danny had ever owned a dog before, the only thing that they could come up with was to get her a bowl of water.

Both boys sat next to her on the floor, speaking softly. The attic was stifling with the heat and Marin the dog was panting.

Slam went the front door shaking the entire house. Josh looked at Danny with horror on his face.

"Josh, Marin, I forgot my briefcase," their mom called out to them. "Are you guys still working in the attic?"

"Oh no, you gotta hide! I'll be in such trouble. Oh crap! Hide Marin too. We can't have my mom see her like this." Danny jumped up and went to hide behind a dresser in the corner, wedging himself between it and some boxes. Josh pushed Marin the dog into the space next to Danny and placed boxes in front. They were just in time, as their mom entered the attic.

"Hi honey, how's it going?" she said looking around the room. "Where's Marin?"

"Um, she went to the store to get….milk?" he answered hesitantly, while trying to think of where his sister could possibly be, instead of where she should be.

"Milk?" Mom asked. "I thought we had a full container this morning."

"Oh, then I don't know what she went to get, she just left on her bike a few minutes ago and said she was going to the store," he stammered, trying to cover his mistake.

"Ahhhhh chooo!" Mom sneezed in response. "Ahhhh choooo, ahhhh choooo, ahhhhh choooo!"

"Bless you," Josh replied, his eyes wide.

"Thank you. Oh wow," she said rubbing her nose and sniffling. "There's something up here that's making my allergies go crazy. You guys didn't find a dog in these boxes did you?" she added teasingly.

Josh shook his head no with gusto, afraid to speak. In an effort to avoid looking directly at her, he looked down at his feet. Stifling a gasp, he noticed dog fur clinging to his shorts. To hide it, he slowly tuned his body to angle his leg away from his mom's gaze. He couldn't exactly brush it off at the moment.

"Hmm, maybe I'm allergic to dust now. I don't know what it is, but I'm going back to work, just wanted to see how you were faring," she said as she turned around, doing another quick survey of the room. "Looks like you guys are doing a great job up here, keep up the good work," she said as the door to the attic clicked behind her.

Josh let out his breath. "It's okay Danny. She left. You and Marin can come out now," he said relieved.

Josh moved the boxes so they so they could get out of their hiding spot. Sweat was running in rivulets down Danny's face. "Here, have some water," Josh said handing him a bottle.

"Well, that was fun Josh," Danny said after gulping down the water. "What's next? Shall we take her for a walk?" he added sarcastically.

"Look at this!" he exclaimed as he attempted to brush dog fur off his shirt. His shirt was so soaked with sweat that the fur wouldn't budge.

"Sorry, man. Don't tell Marin she was right though, okay?"

Josh thought back to that day at the beach. "How long was she gone that day at the beach?"

"Like two hours."

"Yeah, that's what I sorta remember. That's probably how long it'll be before she changes back again. You wanna wait with me?"

Danny nodded and sat down on old beat up trunk.

A little while later Josh went downstairs to make them sandwiches. While he was in the kitchen he thought he heard whining at the front door. What is that? Did Marin get out? Josh thought as he opened the door to take a quick peek.

Sitting on the front steps were three dogs. One of them was the large black Labrador that lived a few houses over, another the small white poodle that lived next door that always barked at him, and the third one he didn't recognize. They were just sitting there lined up, waiting to be let in. When the lab took a step toward the door, Josh slammed it shut.

Oh man! What's that all about? He thought as he walked back into the kitchen to finish making lunch.

"Danny, you will never believe what I just saw," Josh said handing his friend a sandwich. "There are three dogs outside trying to get in the house."

"What?" Danny said almost choking. "Why?"

"I don't know why. Maybe they want to meet their new neighbor?"

"That makes no sense. Marin isn't a dog." Danny gave Josh a look that said otherwise.

"Well okay, she's one now, but she won't be one forever." I hope, Josh thought looking at his sister.

Marin was sitting right in front of him, drool running out of her mouth onto the floor. "Yuck Marin, here," Josh said, finally handing her a sandwich. In her eagerness to eat, she nipped his hand. "Hey, those are my fingers," he said, rubbing them. Gulping down the food, Marin the dog stood and gazed up at him expectantly. "No, you can't have mine," Josh said in between bites.

Marin whined a little and looked at Danny.

"You can't have mine either," Danny said finishing his last bite.

Leaning back, Marin swung her back leg up to scratch her ear. Dog fur went flying and started to swirl about the room, courtesy of the fans. Josh and Danny once again laughed loudly at this. It was pretty funny to see Marin doing dog things. "Thank goodness we're up here," Josh said. "Look at all of this hair!"

After sniffing and investigating the entire room, Marin finally lay down and rested her head on her paws, dozing off. And just as quickly as it initially happened, Marin changed back into her human form. It was so seamless and flawless a transition that both boys sat there transfixed. Even after seeing it again, they still couldn't believe it.

Marin sat up with a start.

"Holy crap!" she said.

"You remember?" Josh asked his mouth still hanging open. He hadn't expected her to.

"Yeah, I do. I remember everything," she answered with a big yawn. "And by the way, no fleas and I am housebroken."

"Uh, sorry," Danny muttered as he helped her stand up.

Josh snickered. "Well, it was funny watching you do dog things."

"Let's get out of here," she said. "The heat is killing me."

All three of them left the attic and went downstairs to the cool comfort of the kitchen. They had a lot to talk about.

The first thing Marin did after entering the kitchen was to grab a cold glass of ice water. She needed to adjust her body temperature. Fanning herself with a bit of paper, she sat down at the table and looked at the boys. Neither one of them knew what to say or where to begin.

Marin made a quick call to Amy to come over a.s.a.p. Amy arrived a few minutes later as she lived only a two blocks away. Marin didn't tell her what the emergency was, but Amy could tell by the tone of her voice that something had happened.

"So," Marin began after gulping down her drink and starting on a second one. "It would appear that whenever I get really stressed out and think of an animal, I change into it. That just about sums it up, doesn't it?"

Amy looked at her with disbelief. "You can change into an animal?" she asked scanning the faces in the room.

"Yeah, she can. Danny and I just saw her do it. She changed into a dog and wanted to bite me," Josh's voice trailed off while he thought about it. "But, how can you?" he continued. "I mean really, how can you? It just doesn't make any sense. Has anyone ever heard of this?" he asked looking at Danny, Amy, and Marin. All three shook their heads.

They sat in silence for a few minutes while Amy digested what they'd said.

"Geez, do you think we can find any information about this on the internet?" Marin asked. "I'm not optimistic, but I think we should at least try." Josh shook his head in agreement and ran upstairs. A moment later he returned with his laptop.

Typing the words "shape shifter" into a search engine, they were rewarded with way more information than they ever imagined would be available. "Who knew," Marin said to the group after reading a few passages from a webpage, "that there were so many different legends. Over a dozen cultures have legends about shape shifting. And look at this," she said pointing to one passage that caught her eye. "Maybe this is me," she asked looking up. "The Púca is the name of the Celtic legend of shape shifters."

"And we are Irish and Scottish," Josh answered. "Hey wait, Púca with a P, right?" he asked. "Marin," he said looking around the room. "Where is the book we found in your room with the "P" on it?"

Marin's face lit up as she made the connection. Getting up she joined Josh to look for it. They found the book in the family room. "Now this makes a little bit of sense," she said. "Maybe this is a list of all of the members of our family who were Púca."

"But they can't all be Púca," Josh replied thumbing through the pages. "That seems like a lot of people."

"I don't know Josh," Danny finally answered. Marin wasn't sure if he was in shock or something as this was the first time he had spoken to them since she'd changed back. He was still seated at the table and had hardly moved. Marin and Josh hadn't really noticed that until now.

"Danny, are you alright?" Josh asked.

"I'm not sure. I'm still not even sure what I saw or what happened," he said as he laid his head on the table. Marin and Josh sat down next to him and Josh rested his hand on his friend's shoulder.

"You know I would never have hurt you Danny," Marin replied with a little guilt in her voice. "I got mad. I'm sorry."

And you," she said turning to Josh and changing the subject. "Mom came home. See, see I told you so. Boy did you get lucky," she added shaking her head. If you hadn't broken the rules, I wouldn't have gotten mad in the first place. Hey, I know I have to learn to control my temper, but a little help please."

"Yeah, good luck with that," Josh answered. "You've been saying that for years," he continued trying to diffuse the situation. "It hasn't happened yet."

"Well, I better try a lot harder," Marin answered. "Or what happened today could happen again."

Danny looked at her with a startled expression on his face.

"Or better yet, maybe you guys can help me learn to control the change," Marin added looking at them all expectantly.

"Do you really think you can Marin?" Amy asked.

"I don't know, I mean how can I know unless I try?" Marin replied.

"I wonder what kinds of animals you can change into," Josh asked. "There's so much information we don't know."

"And I wonder if there are any more Púca out there," Danny added.

"That would be cool," Marin said. "Heck, I could use all the help with this I can get."

"Well, it looks like we have a mission this summer guys," Josh said looking at the group. "We have to help Marin and make sure no else finds out."

"I think this is going to be one wild summer," Amy said as she walked around the table and hugged Marin. Marin yawned a great wide yawn.

Between the heat of the attic and the change into the dog, she once again desperately needed a nap.

While Marin went upstairs to nap, Josh, Danny, and Amy quickly did a few more things in the attic to make up for the lost work time. Looking around, Amy could see the evidence that a dog had been there. Dog hair was still swirling around in the corners of the room, pushed around by the fans. All three kids got to work. When they did what they thought was enough to satisfy requirements for the day, Amy and Danny left. They certainly didn't want to get caught at the house.

Chapter 8

Josh went to bed that night thinking he'd probably have nightmares about what happened that day. Marin had gotten up from her nap and seemed to be fine, not a care in the world. It just took a physical toll on her and she needed to rest afterwards. Josh was the one who was edgy and nervous. What if she changed again and other people saw? What would they do to Marin if that happened? Would she ever be able to control it, especially with that temper of hers? How often could she change anyway? Was it once a month or anytime she got ticked off or upset? Josh had too many questions going on his mind to be able to relax and sleep. He also wanted to know why it was happening to her and not to him. How cool would that be to be able to change into an animal? Josh tossed and turned as he lay in bed and thought about it. Why does she get to be the special one? He didn't like feeling this way, but he couldn't help it. He was anxious about Marin, but conflicted. It took him hours to fall asleep that night.

The next morning he still wasn't happy. They still had work to do on the attic for the next week or so, and he just wasn't in the mood to deal with it. After breakfast and after Mom left for school, Marin and Josh begrudgingly got to work. They wanted to get as much done as possible and do a good job for their parents, but they also needed to talk. Marin and Josh had both hoped that Amy and Danny would be able to go with them on the camping trip, but they weren't sure at this point.

"So, did you come up with any ideas for how you might try to control it?" Josh asked Marin as he absentmindedly brushed dust off one of the numerous boxes he had to take downstairs.

"Not at all," she replied without looking up from the boxes she was stacking. They'd cleaned up the dog hair yesterday, and the three kids had done a bunch of work, but there was still plenty to do. "It almost seems like we're playing with fire. What if something goes wrong and I wind up hurting someone?" Marin asked aloud, not really expecting any kind of answer from her brother.

"The only thing that I can think of, is for you to not get mad," Josh said to his sister with a glint of mischief in his eye. He knew that sometimes it was like speaking to a brick wall when it came to her temper, but he said it anyway.

Marin looked up from her work and glared at him. "What, you think I like to lose my temper and go all ballistic? I don't think so."

"Well, you're definitely going to have to try harder now, aren't you? Or the whole world will know your secret."

"What do you recommend?" She answered with a small challenge in her voice.

"Well, for one thing...how about the old standby of counting to ten, to help relieve the stress and tension?" he offered.

Marin thought about this for a few seconds, before she nodded in agreement. "The trouble will be when I forget to do that," she said smiling. "You don't understand what happens to me when I get really mad. I literally see red and cannot control myself."

"You forget," Josh countered. "I have been trying to learn to control myself since I was a little kid. The ADHD I have sucks. I have been dealing with what you're going through my whole life. It's gonna take practice and some help from me, Amy, and Danny. But I think you can do it if you try."

"I guess time will tell, won't it. I'll either be able to control my anger, or I won't," Marin added with a shrug. "And what about if I get emotional? I can't even begin to think about that. That's gonna be even harder to deal with. The only consolation is that that doesn't happen as often as my bad temper does.... yet."

****

The next two weeks were uneventful as Marin and Josh cleaned out the attic and generally did their best to behave. None of the kids were sure they wanted to see Marin change again and no one encouraged her to try. It was scary enough the first time they saw it. Amy was still skeptical and Danny did his best to pretend it never happened.

Mom and Dad made sure that Marin and Josh did laps at the local pool every day after their chores were done. Marin would have liked nothing better than to curl up with a good book and relax. Instead, they had to deal with the crowds at the pool. Josh relished this part of the day more than Marin, and did his best to improve his speed. Even though he had gotten a cramp that day at the beach, he had been trailing behind. The fact that Marin had won the race had irked him to no end. And she had started from behind!

The morning they were to set out for their camping trip, Josh was still worried about his sister. But he was also hesitant to talk to her. It felt a bit like living with a walking time bomb, not knowing when it might go off. He felt powerless to help her, while simultaneously jealous of her ability. And to make matters worse, Amy and Danny were not going with them on the camping trip.

They were only able to rent a small motor home that slept five, and not the bigger one they needed to be able to take along two extra kids. Both Josh and Danny had volunteered to pitch a tent, but Mom wouldn't hear of it. So it looked like Josh was on his own watching out for his sister while they were away.

Mom and Dad decided their destination was going to be a national park in Virginia. With a huge bunch of luck, they managed to get a reservation at one of the bigger campgrounds due to a last minute cancellation. Hiking, biking, fishing, and looking for wildlife were going to be the order of the day. The best part according to Mom and Dad, would be the lack of internet, cell phones etc. that they would not be able to have while visiting the park. Not only that, but no electricity or running water either. They would have to retrieve water and run the generator in the motor home to cook. The campground did provide showers though, Marin was relieved to find. It also had a laundry room and a camp store. No pool though, Marin saw while she checked online before they left. But their campground was near three waterfalls and a beautiful meadow with plenty of wildlife and plants. Mapping it out, she calculated that would take about ten hours of driving to get there from Florida.

Marin and Josh weren't too concerned about the lack of cell phones or internet service. They knew that they wouldn't be able to watch TV, as the camper was not equipped with one. So instead they packed an old portable DVD player. Josh brought his hand held video game along while Marin brought a few books she'd been dying to read. They also had a small assortment of board games to help quell the boredom of the long drives there and back.

The trip up to Virginia was tedious to Josh. You can only play so many video games and watch DVD's for so long. Marin on the other hand was thrilled to be able to spend all of her time glued to a book. Mom and Dad alternated driving and resting. They stopped a couple of times during the day to get gas and have meals.

Pulling into the park, both kids were amazed at the size of the place. Pictures and descriptions on the internet didn't do it justice. The park encompasses hundreds of thousands of acres and has five hundred miles of trails. Their campground was located about half way through. There were over two hundred campsites at their campground and almost every one of them was occupied when they pulled in. Some areas were for tents only while others could accommodate motor homes like theirs. Mom and Dad printed a few brochures and maps from the website so they knew where they were going and where to park as neither of them had been there before. The campground even had an amphitheater and a Lodge where you could get breakfast, lunch, and dinner if you wanted. Plus during the evenings, Park Rangers held programs on the wonders of the park.

Before they even finished parking the motor home, Josh was bouncing up and down just itching to be outside and go exploring. He was antsy from sitting all day. Marin was too, although she didn't show it as much as he did.

"Mom, Dad, can I go exploring?" Josh begged as soon as Dad turned the ignition off.

"Yeah, me too," Marin piped in looking up from her book.

"Okay, you two," Mom answered. "You can go and look around, but stay together. We don't know the lay of the land around here yet and it's dusk already. I want you guys back here in one hour. And remember where we parked!"

"We're just going to walk around the campground and see where everything is. We'll be back in an hour, promise," Marin replied for both of them as she exited the camper. Josh came bounding out with two flashlights in hand and handed one to Marin. Marin quickly checked her map and saw where they were parked in relation to the general store. Even though it was summer, it felt a little chilly to Marin. After they had only been walking a few minutes, she shivered. Mental note to self, summer nights in Virginia are nippy, bring along a jacket, Marin thought.

Their campsite was at the north end of the campground and interestingly enough, right near one of the entrances to the Appalachian Trail. Unfortunately, that also meant that they had to do a bit of walking to get to the store. When they got there, Marin was grateful that she had plenty of money on her. She decided right then and there to purchase a hoodie for the walk back to the camper. She was chilled to the bone. Josh would never part with his money for a sweatshirt. He was just too into video games at this point and most of his money went there. Marin also bought a guide book of the park while she was there.

There were so many kids at this campground, Josh was actually at a loss as to whether to talk to any of them. While most of them were younger than they were, Josh saw a handful of them that might be around their age.

The Lodge, located near the general store seemed to be the place to be. Since it served hot food as well as being a hotel, there was a constant stream of people going in and out. Marin and Josh didn't have the luxury of hanging around though, because they had to head back to the RV camper as their hour was almost up.

Mom chuckled to herself when she saw what Marin was wearing when they arrived back. She'd held her tongue when the twins left earlier. She wanted to tell them to wear jackets, but had a feeling she would have met with resistance, so she didn't say anything.

While Marin and Josh were gone, Dad started the barbeque. The grill sizzled with the sound of burgers and hotdogs cooking. Josh made a beeline for the rolls and filled his plate barely remembering to thank his dad.

Marin had picked up a schedule at the camp store for the Amphitheater. She was interested in so many things, she didn't know where to start. Mom settled that one. They would start out with an easy Ranger led hike tomorrow. Later in the week they would try some of the tougher trails, if Mom and

Dad thought they could handle them. Marin was ecstatic about that and couldn't wait to start taking tons of pictures.

****

The family quickly settled into a routine. Every morning after breakfast they did some kind of hiking. Sometimes the treks were short and sometimes they lasted most of the day. After the first short Ranger led trek, Mom and Dad got adventurous and decided they would tackle the other hikes on their own. There were so many to choose from that they were able to go on a different hiking path each day. Some were short and scenic and some were steep climbs that required stamina. Josh didn't care where they went, as long as it was some place new. Both kids made it a game to see who could spot the most wild-life along the way. And of course, Marin did her best to document their hikes with her camera by taking as many pictures as she could.

Josh and Marin each managed to make a friend. They'd attended a Bird of Prey Ranger lecture program and a lot of the kids staying at their camp ground were there. Josh was pleased that he now had a guy friend to hang around with after their hikes. As much as he loved his family, that rented RV camper was small. It's not like living in a house where everyone has their own room. So it was nice to be able to hang out with his new friend Bruce at the lodge or general store and talk about video games.

Marin didn't like Bruce. He seemed a bit of a jerk. He was always talking about how much money his family had and all of the video games that he owned. Marin was glad she didn't have to spend too much time in his company. Besides, she'd made a new friend too by the name of Jessie.

Much to Marin's horror and eventual amusement, Josh really liked her new friend Jessie. She'd had a crush on Chris Avery for the better part of the school year which Josh teased her about all the time. But now it was her brother's turn. It quickly became pretty obvious to their parents too. He was always hanging around when she and Jessie met up, even inviting himself along when they went to get ice cream in the evenings.

Marin didn't care though. They were on vacation. It's not like they were going to see their new friends much (if ever) after they left to go back home. Jessie and her brothers lived in Maryland.

Marin was having trouble getting used to Jessie's younger brothers. Such little pests! They were 6 and 7 years old and constantly fighting. It drove Marin crazy. Marin was in awe of her new friend and the patience she showed to her brothers. They wanted to go anywhere Jessie went; it didn't matter on the destination.

How do you talk to your new friend about boys and stuff when you have two little brothers hanging around all the time? It frustrated Marin, but she really couldn't say anything to Jessie about it.

Most nights when they got back to the campsite, Marin and Jessie would walk over to the general store for ice cream. It almost always turned into a small party with Bruce, Josh, and Jessie's younger brothers Jack and Jimmy tagging along.

But Marin had to admit that this trip was fun. She'd been hesitant at first to go camping, but quickly got over it. The daily hikes took care of that. There were some evenings when they got back from their hikes that she was so tired, she fell into bed. They were so busy exploring the park and enjoying themselves that Marin and Josh both temporarily forgot about Marin's little problem.

All of that changed though on the morning of their fifth day. The kids had been pestering their parents and insisting that they all go together on a group hike. So after much discussion among the parents, the group chose a moderate hike that wouldn't be too difficult because of Jessie's younger brothers.

"Mom," Josh said as they were getting ready that morning. "How much water do you think I should bring along today?" Josh made sure to ask every morning about the water. He got into the habit after the first hike when he discovered he hadn't brought enough along. The family shared theirs with him, but he vowed to himself not to let it happen again. He figured it was better to have too much than not enough. He hadn't known that drinking water from a stream could make you sick unless it was boiled first.

"Fill up all of your canteens today Josh," Mom replied casually. Marin looked up from her book and gazed at her mom. The sun had tanned her a bit and she positively glowed. Dad was helping her with the sandwiches and he kept trying to sneak her a kiss. Marin rolled her eyes as this...geez. Did they have to do that in front of her?

Marin put away her book and got her canteens filled as well. Marin was happy that they were finally all going to go hiking together, even though the little kids and Bruce would be with them.

Checking her camera bag, she was thankful she had one unused memory card left. She thought she might fill it up today.

Both Josh and Marin each had a small back pack they used to keep their gear in. They carried snacks and each had a folded portable raincoat. The bags weren't too heavy, which was good because once they added their filled canteens, they would be.

Josh was bouncing up and down a bit in the trailer and it started rocking a bit. Dad sent Josh outside to see how the other families were faring. They were all supposed to meet up at 9 am at the north end of the campground and pick up the Appalachian Trail. Jessie's family was camped closest to them, so Josh headed over there.

Jessie's whole family was gathered around their picnic table discussing food options when Josh walked over and joined them. Josh was pleased when Jessie watched him arrive and gave him a small smile.

"Where's Marin?" she asked when he sat down opposite her.

"She's still getting ready. My dad sent me on ahead to see how everyone was coming along," Josh replied shyly gazing at her.

As usual, Jessie's little brothers were bickering about something. Josh tried to ignore them, but that didn't work out very well. Once they saw him, they stopped arguing and ran over to see him. Marin arrived at Jessie's family campsite at that point, camera in hand.

"Hey everyone...picture time," she said loudly. "Everybody stand or sit in front of the picnic table so I can get a good shot." No one was paying her any attention, so she took a candid photo of the group getting ready. The younger boys were trying to get Josh's attention and all Josh wanted to do was talk to Jessie. Marin just shook her head and gave up. When she started walking toward the trail entrance, the rest of them got up and followed her. By the time they got to the starting sign, Marin and Josh's parents were waiting for them there.

Bruce was waiting for them to tell them that he and his family wouldn't be joining them. Marin did her best not to smile at the news. Both of his parents had overdone it the day before and decided not to do the hike today. Instead of hiking, Bruce was headed toward another Ranger lecture that morning.

So, are we ready for this gang?" Jessie's dad called out. "Let's do it."

"Yeah!" both of Jessie's brothers answered simultaneously. Josh laughed. This hike is gonna be fun, Josh thought. Even if those two kids aggravate me, I won't let them spoil the day for me.

Marin was pretty much thinking the same thing. The boys were pests, but mostly to Josh. I hope we get to see some new wild life today. If they ruin it, I'm going to be ticked off. As she thought this, Marin thought of a game that they used to play when they were younger and she and Josh were fighting in the car. Her dad would start off with, "Silence in the court house, the monkey wants to speak... speak, monkey, speak!" The point of the game was to keep the kids as quiet as possible and the first one to speak would lose the game and be "the monkey." Even if one of the kids broke the silence by speaking and lost the game, it was always good for getting laughs. The game may not last too long, but at least they would have some peace and quiet for a bit while they hiked.

After several hours of easy hiking and snack and water breaks, the group stopped for lunch. Skirting around the base of a small mountain, they'd emerged from the woods and discovered a breathtaking meadow filled with colorful flowers and a stream running through it. At least that was what the map said was supposed to be there. The reality was a bit different. It'd rained heavily every night during the past few weeks and combined with water running off from the snow on top of the mountain, the stream now looked like a small river.

It was quite pretty, Marin reflected as she surveyed the landscape and took photos. The monkey game had lasted only about a half an hour, which wasn't long enough as far as Marin was concerned. The chatty little boys had scared most of the wild life away. Josh had spent the entirety of their walk right next to Marin and Jessie, with the younger boys trailing as close behind as they could, constantly asking about video games and sports.

Marin was happy that Josh liked her friend. She was sweet and kind, especially with her brothers. While they walked, she told them that the boys also had ADHD. They had just been diagnosed and were going to start therapy and meds when they got home. That explained why they were very hyper and as bouncy as ping pong balls, Marin thought. Had Josh been like this when he was younger? Marin couldn't remember. What she did know was that Josh hadn't taken any of his medicine while they had been on this camping trip.

They set up their picnic lunch facing the stream, placing blankets down so they could relax and enjoy the view for an hour or so. The plan was to start back to camp after lunch.

Jessie talked Josh into taking a little stroll while she picked some flowers. The little boys wanted nothing to do with picking flowers and instead decided to check out the stream looking for frogs.

Jessie's mom called to them, "Jack, Jimmy, keep your distance from that water!"

"Jessie, can you keep an eye on them please?"

Jessie waived to her mom while nodding her head. The boys then busied themselves with a game of tag. Marin couldn't believe they still had so much energy left.

Marin was amused when she noticed what Jessie and Josh were doing in the field. While collecting the flowers, somehow they wound up holding hands. Payback time, Marin thought. Zooming her camera lens, she sneakily took photos of them. When she was done, she joined all of the parents on the blankets and grabbed herself a sandwich and plopped her back pack down. Looking up from her meal, she could see the boys laughing and running around. They appeared to be having a grand old time.

Holding a huge bouquet of wildflowers, Jessie and Josh crossed the waist high field of grass and flowers and began to follow the stream to meet up with the boys. When they got about fifty feet from them, they both stopped dead in their tracks.

The boys were feeding a bear cub and playing with it. It was black and the size of a dog. It had been impossible to see from a distance due to its size and the height of the grass.

Jessie let out a small gasp under her breath and Josh scanned the area quickly, a panicked expression on his face. Grabbing Jessie by the arm, he pointed at the edge of the woods. Approaching at a gallop behind the boys was the mother bear.

"Jack, Jimmy, look!" Josh screamed. "Stop what you're doing immediately! Walk quickly to us, but don't turn your back on the bear!" Both boys turned and looked behind them in the direction that Josh was pointing. But instead of freezing in their tracks and backing away from the baby bear like Josh asked, panic set in. Turning to their left, they ran directly toward the overflowing stream. Seeing them as prey, the mother bear altered her direction, right toward them. They shrieked an ear piercing, bone rattling scream and started to run blindly along the edge of the stream as fast as their little legs would carry them toward Josh and Jessie. Their shriek scared the baby bear which turned and ran toward the trees, but it didn't stop the mother bear.

"No, stop running!" Jessie yelled, waiving her arms. But it was too late. Josh and Jessie reacted immediately by running toward the boys too. Josh didn't know what he could do, but he had to try.

By this time, all of the parents including Marin were now running full speed toward them as well. They couldn't see what was going on, but they heard the high pitched scream of the little boys and they'd reacted.

Jessie's parents had brought pepper spray as a precaution against bears. The trouble was that there was a huge distance between the parents and the little boys. Of course you had to be close to a bear to use it, and they weren't going to get to the little kids first.

The mother bear quickly closed the distance to the boys. With a rake of her paw, she swiped at Jimmy who was closest to her. Her paw made contact with the pack on his back and propelled him forward, right into his brother. Both boys landed in the water with a splash and were immediately swept away by the current.

"Oh my gosh! Do something! Help, Help!" Jessie screamed, flailing her arms.

Without thinking, Josh executed his best swim team dive into the cold water after them. Unfortunately he forgot that he was still wearing his back pack. It cut into his shoulder as he hit the water. But he didn't even give it a moment's notice as he now had to fight to stay afloat and keep his head above water. The current had not appeared to be strong when looking at the stream, but clearly it was. Josh said a silent prayer for the boys.

Jessie's blood curdling scream and arm flailing had stopped the mother bear in her tracks. It stood on the edge of the river snarling at her, but didn't pursue the boys. By now, all of the parents and Marin were within visual range as well. They slowed down their approach and began waving their arms and shouting as they cautiously approached Jessie by the edge of the stream. Both of Jessie's parents had their pepper sprays at the ready in case the bear charged again. But seeing the large group of people approach, the startled mother bear turned around and fled in the direction her baby had gone.

"Jessie, where are the boys?" her Dad asked, as he scanned the area.

"The bear!" Jessie answered, barely able to speak.

"Where's Josh?" Marin's mom questioned as well, a look of worry on her face as she looked around for him.

"He dove in to save them," Jessie whispered in awe.

There was no sign of any of the boys. No one spoke, they were all too shocked. Then Marin's Dad turned around and started running back toward their gear on the blankets. They all turned and ran, following him. Back at the blankets they hastily packed up their gear and all of them tried to use their cell phones to call for help. But it was no use. No one was able to get a signal.

"We need a plan," Jessie's mom said. "We need to split up and start searching for them. Someone also needs to go get help from the Rangers." To her husband she asked, "Joe, since I'm the better hiker, why don't you go get help with Jessie? I'll follow the stream as best as I can."

"I'll go with you," Marin's mom answered. "My son is out there too." They quickly split up their gear. Both of the moms made sure that each group had a map, a compass, plus water and the mostly uneaten lunch. Jessie's dad even surprised them by pulling flares from his pack and giving them to his wife.

"I don't know if these will do any good, but take them anyway," he said.

Jessie wanted to protest and volunteer to look as well, but she thought better of it. Her parents must be stressed enough, without her adding to it. Instead, she hugged her mom, and wished both of them good luck as they started off at a fast walk toward the edge of the stream and began following it.

"Where is the nearest Ranger station Dad?" Marin asked.

"Is it close by?" Jessie's dad wondered.

"It looks like there's one a few miles from here. Let's go."

Marin reached over and grabbed Jessie by her shoulders and looked her in the eyes. Jessie's eyes had begun to fill with tears. "Don't worry Jess. Our moms will find them. Let's go and get them some help." With a quick reassuring hug, Marin and

Jessie turned and followed their dads as they started their trek to the Ranger station.

****

The current was swift and silent as it carried the boys and Josh downstream from the meadow. Josh could barely make them out bobbing up and down before the stream started a series of turns and twists. A few minutes later he saw the water moving around a huge boulder up ahead. And the stream, which was more of a mini-river, split in two different directions at its base. Oh crap, he thought. Which way should I try to go? Josh had only seconds to make a decision. He tried to take the fork to the right, but the current was too strong and it forced him to take the split to the left. Silently cursing, he scanned the water looking for the kids a few hundred feet later when the stream straightened out again. Incredibly, the current started to pick up again at this point. Did they make it out? he wondered doing his best to see them. Did I just float past them and miss them? Josh craned his neck to scout the water ahead of him for the boys, but saw nothing.

What seemed like miles later, Josh miraculously saw a fallen tree trunk up ahead. It was acting like a small dam with branches, twigs, leaves and such getting trapped in front of it. Using what little energy he had left, he angled himself toward it and was rewarded when it snagged him. Unfortunately, storm debris began collecting there with him as well while he was pressed up against it and it started hitting him. It took all of his remaining reserve of energy to hold onto the tree and pull himself along to the edge of the river bank. He tried to stand up, but quickly fell back down. His legs were like jelly from being in the water and fighting the current. Oh my gosh, those poor kids, he thought. If this is how I feel and I'm a swimmer, I can't imagine what they must feel like. I hope they're okay. Josh lay there on the muddy bank for a few minutes. Gradually, he made his way into a sitting position and looked around to see if he could tell where he was. Looking up, he noticed the position of the sun in the sky. It was getting low. Too bad I was never a boy scout, he thought to himself as he once again tried to stand up. Then maybe I would be able to navigate a bit and find the boys and our way back to civilization. Josh could barely lift his legs and put them down again, but he managed to stand up.

It was at this point that he remembered the pack on his back. Pulling it off, he inspected its contents to see if he had lost anything. While everything was soaking wet, all of the items inside were still there. He had a small length of rope, matches, three energy bars, a light jacket, and his water canteens. The matches and energy bars were in sealed containers and hadn't gotten wet, he was thankful to see. He hadn't thought to bring a compass or any kind of map, as his dad had carried those items. He also didn't have any band aids or bandages for the cut on his shoulder that was now throbbing, reminding Josh that it was there. He tied the jacket to the outside of the pack to air it out and dry, and put the pack back on, wincing a bit when it touched the cut on his shoulder again.

Gulping some of the water from his bottle, Josh listened in the woods for any noise from the boys. All he could hear was the water rushing by him. Great, he thought to himself. Now I'm lost too.

And I have absolutely no idea where I am, or worse, where the boys are.

****

Marin, Jessie, and their fathers made it to the Ranger Station in a little under an hour. It was at the Ranger station that they all found out how deadly the water in the park could be after heavy rains. Notice had gone out that morning, but they'd left the campground too early to have heard about it. Not that they had been planning on doing any swimming or anything in the water, but it would have been nice to know. Although how can you predict that a mother black bear and her cub would change all of that, Marin thought to herself. Marin had read that black bears do their best to avoid people, unless you feed them. And the boys had been feeding and playing with the cub. That's not something that happens often either. And everyone knows that a mother bear protecting her cubs can be dangerous.

Marin was beginning to feel like she was cursed or jinxed or something. What has been going on this summer anyway? It's been crazy. At least this time it isn't me who's lost. Those poor boys! I hope they can find them.

The Rangers took action immediately and summoned all of the other Ranger Stations to help with whatever personnel they could spare. Search teams would search on a grid of the park from the last known position the boys had been seen. They were using All Terrain vehicles and some of them even had horses for the hard to reach areas that a motorized vehicle wouldn't be able to get to.

Marin, Jessie and their fathers were taken by jeep back to their camp ground to wait for news. They were strictly instructed not to go looking themselves. But it was too late for that as the moms were out looking. They made sure that the Rangers knew that. At least both of them were experienced at hiking. While neither of them had any kind of tracking experience that Marin knew about, they could read a map and a compass and get around okay. Marin was doing her best to be optimistic.

****

Caitlyn Royce and Jennifer Hodges had been walking for hours and were frustrated. They had not seen any sign of the three boys, not one. And to make matters worse, they had reached the part of the stream where the boulder cut it into two directions and they were forced to stay to the right of it. They certainly could not risk trying to cross it, as they knew they would be taken with the current as well. So even if they had wanted to split up, they couldn't. They had to just keep following the water and looking for foot prints at its edge to see if they could find the boys. Of course they had been calling out to the boys as well, but it didn't matter. If the boys had managed to get out of the water, they could have wandered off and gone anywhere.

By this time, they were both extremely tired and the sun was going to go down shortly. The food was running low and they were almost out of fresh water. Unless they wanted to stop and boil some, they were going to have to make a decision whether to continue on, stop and camp overnight, or head back to their campground and wait for the Rangers. For all they knew, the boys had been found already. Neither one of them would say aloud what they were also thinking, that maybe one or all of them had drowned. In Caitlyn's mind, that just wasn't going to be an option. Both moms were determined to find their sons, alive.

****

Josh had started walking along the river after a rest of about thirty minutes or so. He had eaten one of the snack bars and that helped a lot. He wanted to save the other two for the boys, but he didn't know if he would be able to. Every few minutes or so he would call out to them, but he never got an answer back. He wasn't even sure if he should be searching, as he was pretty much lost too.

When the sun started to go down, Josh knew he needed to find somewhere to stop for the night. He found a spot between a few small pine trees and sat down. He really wanted to eat another energy bar, but forced himself not to. He was low on water as well and needed to conserve that. I'm sure there are Rangers out looking for me and the boys by now, he hoped.

****

Marin and her dad went back to the camper to wait for news. Jessie and her dad went back to their tent to do the same thing. There wasn't much to do, but worry and wait. As a diversion from the tension she felt, Marin sat on her bed, picked up one of her books and started to read. She needed to occupy her mind with something else. She knew what could happen and she couldn't risk anyone seeing her change into an animal, even if she wanted to. Thankfully the book did its job and within a few minutes, Marin dozed off.

An hour later, Marin was rudely awakened by shouting from outside. Jessie was at the door. Both moms had returned. It had broken their hearts to do so, but in the end it seemed the wisest choice. They had run out of water and could barely walk anymore from the day's exertions.

Meanwhile, the Rangers sent a messenger to Dad to give him an update. They were suspending the search until morning. Blood hounds were to be brought in to help as well, and they would start again at daybreak. No one was happy about that, but what could they do? It is almost impossible to search at night, especially for small boys like Jimmy and Jack. They would be very hard to spot. Both families agreed that the only thing they could do now was wait until morning and go to bed. No one expected to get much sleep.

****

Josh had only been sleeping a few hours when he awoke with a start. The sound of twigs snapping nearby had alerted him to something or someone approaching. He lay on his makeshift bed of pine needles frozen with fear. What if it was another bear or worse? He really wished that he had studied up a bit on all of the possible types of wildlife that were found in the park like Marin had done. He stayed there quietly listening until he couldn't hear it moving around anymore. Relieved and annoyed, Josh sat up and began shoving his gear in his small day pack.

What a fool I've been, thinking I could save those boys! I'm not a tracker or experienced in search and rescue. But how can I go back and face Jessie if I don't find her brothers! I'm lost and they're lost, and now we all need rescuing. What we need is for Marin to save us by changing into a blood hound or wolf or something, he thought, his anger and frustration rising by the second. If only I could do that too! I could find them fast!

"AHHHHHHHH," Josh screamed into the woods with everything he had, his anger and frustration now having reached a peak he couldn't control. Taking another deep breath, he tried screaming again but couldn't. His pack slipped out of his hand and landed with a quiet thud. Josh looked down with confusion and fascination. His hand was rippling with fur. His fingers were disappearing one by one and being replaced with claws. Within seconds his hand was replaced by a paw. This is cool! he thought as he dropped to his knees, his back arching up, the transformation completing itself. Just as swiftly as Marin had changed into a dog, Josh became a full grown 140-pound gray wolf.

Lifting his snout into the air and inhaling deeply, Wolf-Josh let out a howl, "a-wooooooooooooooo!" silencing the night creatures for miles around. Wolf-Josh was elated as he jumped around on all four legs doing a wolf version of a dance of joy. He could find the boys now! Wolves have an incredible sense of smell. This is going to be a piece of cake, Wolf-Josh thought as he picked up his day pack with his mouth. Hmm, he hadn't thought about having to carrying the pack in his mouth, but too late now. Moving as fast as he could, he made his way back to the river to start the search over again.

Wolf-Josh made good time getting back, but he was thirsty. Dipping his head into the refreshing water, he lapped up as much as he could. He hoped he didn't get sick, but there wasn't a choice. He had saved the water in the canteens for the boys. Besides, he couldn't open it now even if he wanted to without fingers and thumbs.

Wolf-Josh lifted his long nose into the air and inhaled deeply. Wolves can smell game for miles. They also have an incredible sense of hearing. Those boys were always fighting and if they weren't unconscious, they should be easy to find with my new ears and nose he thought. He didn't know what he would do if they were injured and needed medical care though. How would he be able to lead them back to the campsite that way?

He wasn't even sure they wouldn't freak out at the sight of a wolf. Most people would, but he had to try anyway. Besides, maybe they would think he was just a really big dog, they were little kids after all. I just hope they aren't afraid of dogs, he grimaced as he thought about what to do next.

He hadn't picked up their scent in the wind with his nose, so Wolf-Josh tried a new tactic. He put his nose near the edge of the river and began to trot. He looked a little silly running with the pack in his mouth, but it couldn't be helped. He knew enough about dehydration to know that without water, those boys didn't stand a chance. He also hoped that they hadn't been desperate enough to try drinking from the river.

Thankfully it hadn't rained last night and the river had receded a bit. Wolf-Josh continued running along the bank until his keen eyes spotted something. Wolf-Josh froze in his tracks, gently dropping his pack in the soft squishy mud oozing between his paws. A small gray rabbit was fifteen feet in front of him, lapping up water.

Crouching down, wolf instinct took over. His nose twitched in response to the hunger inducing presence of the rabbit, the predator in him barely controllable.

His stomach growled. The rabbit heard him and looked up, their eyes briefly meeting. The blood in Wolf-Josh's head began to pound as the adrenaline surged through his body. The poor rabbit sensed the danger and leapt into the woods, running at lightning speed. Wolf-Josh bolted after it, all four paws slipping in the mud. But it was no use.

The rabbit won. It easily zigged and zagged to avoid Wolf-Josh's feeble attempt to catch it. But that didn't stop him from trying. Round and round the trees, in and out of bushes, Wolf-Josh finally had to concede defeat and give up. He was scratched, bruised and bleeding courtesy of some sticker bushes and his own lack of coordination. It was one thing to have the body and senses of a wolf, it was another thing to be able to use it.

Panting hard, tongue hanging out of his mouth, Wolf-Josh made his way back to the river to collect his pack and have another drink. What was I thinking chasing that rabbit, he thought as he made his way back, retracing his steps. How much time did I lose chasing it? And what would I have done once I caught it? Eat it? Would I really have killed and eaten a raw rabbit? Yuck! I gotta get a grip on this....focus Josh! Focus! You can do this. You can find those boys.

Wolf-Josh picked up his pack and began to trot along the edge of the bank again, on the lookout for any sign of the boys. He was rewarded a short while later when his keen eyesight noticed a branch dangling with a small piece of ripped clothing stuck to it. It must have been pulled off someone's shirt or pants as they walked near it. Wolf-Josh inhaled deeply. This has to be them! Scanning the ground for footprints, he saw two sets of small footprints walking off into the woods. Once again Wolf-Josh angled his head up and took a deep breath to get a sense of direction for the boys or whoever belonged to the scrap of fabric he'd just found.

Sunlight was peering over the small hill to the east and a strong breeze was stirring the tops of the trees as Wolf-Josh started running at full speed toward the scent, the pack bouncing up and down as he galloped through the woods. At least I'm getting a little better at this wolf stuff, he thought. I haven't crashed or slipped for a while now.

When he got to within a quarter mile or so of them, he started to hear them arguing. Yes, it's them! He couldn't believe what he was hearing!

Here they are lost in the woods, probably cold and hungry and they are yelling at each other at the top of their voices. Well, some things will never change he thought, with a slight change of direction now that he had a better fix on their position.

Wolf-Josh reached the boys five minutes later and thought about the best way to approach them and not frighten them. Wagging his tail a bit like a dog would, Wolf-Josh approached the boys slowly. When he saw their startled looks, he quickly added in whimpering and lowered his body as close to the ground as he could while still moving. He hoped that carrying the pack in his mouth would help quell their fear. I mean how many wolves, or dogs for that matter, would approach someone in the woods with a back pack in their mouth?

By the time Wolf-Josh was within twenty feet of them, he was practically crawling toward them on all fours. As a wolf, he could feel the tension in their bodies. Even though it was a chilly morning, the boys were sweating and clutching each other, their eyes wide with fear as they watched him approach. And for once they were silent; Wolf-Josh noticed. As he crept closer, he could see them visibly relax as soon as they saw the pack in his mouth. When he got to within five feet of them, he lay down and rolled a bit on his side so that his belly was exposed in a form of submission. Dogs and wolves both do this, Josh had observed watching videos of them on the internet. Right after Marin had changed into a dog, Josh got busy and looked up some facts about them. He didn't want to be caught unprepared in case she changed again. Both boys were astonished, but Josh's plan worked. He had to admit that knowing just a little bit about how dogs behave had been crucial at this point, especially since he was twice the size of an average dog.

The boys remained quiet and were watching wolf-Josh expectantly. He slowly got up and approached them, panting hard. Because of the running and crawling, he was tired. With a flip of his head, he flung the pack toward their feet. They boys looked at each other, grabbed the pack, and immediately started fighting over the snacks and water. Geez, Wolf-Josh thought, really? Again?

After they stuffed their faces and finished off the water, Wolf-Josh looked in the direction of where he wanted them to go, and then looked back at the boys. His best bet he thought, would be to head back toward the water. He did this a few times, looking in the direction he wanted them to go, and then back to them. He also added in a bit of a wolfie whine for added emphasis. His ploy worked. He started to walk away from them toward the mini-river, and they quickly followed. I guess they don't want to be alone anymore he thought. I don't blame them. The woods can be a scary place for anyone, especially little kids alone.

They formed a small triangle procession with Wolf-Josh in the lead and the boys on either side of him, clutching onto his fur. They must be cold, he thought, for them to be gripping him so tightly. And I guess I'm radiating enough heat for all of us.

It didn't take but a half an hour or so for Wolf-Josh to pick up the scent of hound dogs and a search team. This was going to be the tricky part. He needed to get the boys to safety, but he had to do it without being seen. Wolf-Josh didn't know if there were wolves in this park, but he also didn't want to cause a scene by walking the children to the searchers. He didn't think it would go over too well. Besides, they may want to shoot him or capture him and his mere presence could put the whole park on alert. He certainly didn't want that to happen. And he had to make his way back to safety too. Josh had hoped to be able to change back into himself and approach the Rangers that way, but it was not meant to be.

Once the boys heard the braying of the blood hounds, and the possibility of imminent rescue, they started shouting. The volume of the barking and howling dogs increased dramatically within a few seconds, if that was possible. Uh, oh Wolf-Josh thought. They must smell my scent and it must be driving them crazy. With a slight twist of his body, Wolf-Josh shook off the boys who were still gripping his fur, turned, and ran full speed in the opposite direction trying to put some distance between them. His initial plan was to keep clear of the Rangers and hide until he shifted back into human form. Then he could just join them and everything would be okay. It hadn't occurred to him that the bloodhounds would freak out because of him.

Trying to think of a new plan, Wolf-Josh kept running, making a wide circle around another search team he found along the way. Two miles out, he changed direction once again when he caught the whiff of a campfire. Someone with a permit must be doing a deep overnight camp he realized. He needed to locate them so he could get back to his family. He didn't know how long he had been a wolf, but he figured he had from two to three hours before he changed back, like Marin had. How long had it been? He didn't know, so he plopped himself down in the brush a short distance from the campers and kept a close eye on them. In the meantime, he kept his ears and nose on the alert for any more search teams and their dogs. He could see and smell that they were cooking breakfast. Oh yes, he thought, his mouth drooling all over his paws, waiting for the change to happen. Please leave me some, he thought as his stomach growled; reminding him that he hadn't eaten much for the last twenty-four hours.

****

The sun peaked in the window of the dimly lit sleeping area that was Marin's part of the camper. Shielding her eyes, she sat up and groggily looked around. She didn't know where she was. "Hello," she called out tentatively, hoping someone she knew would answer her.

"What is it Marin?" her dad answered, pulling back the curtain to see her.

"What's going on? Where are we?" she asked clutching her head, looking around, not sure of what was going on.

"Are you all right?" he asked, as he reached out to feel her forehead for fever. "We're on a camping trip in Virginia and your brother and your friend Jessie's little brothers went missing yesterday while we were hiking. You don't remember that?" he quizzed her, while motioning to Caitlyn to come over to them.

"Huh?" she replied, confusion still evident in her voice as she looked from her father to her mother. "We're camping and Josh is missing? Aw man, my head hurts."

She'd just been dreaming of being a wolf. Marin held her head and put it back down on her pillow, while dad went to fetch a cold wet cloth. She needed to focus and think. The images of her dream were still swelling around in her mind and hadn't stopped when she woke up. It was as if they

131

were happening to her now and not in a dream. It was hard to think. She was in the camper, but she was also running through the woods, panting hard. She could hear dogs barking and yowling off in the distance. She could smell wood burning and food cooking. It was all so disorienting that she was glad she was lying down. How can she be here and there at the same time? This wasn't making any sense, I'm awake now, she thought. Why does it feel like I'm still dreaming?

Thankfully the sensation of being a wolf in the woods only lasted a few more minutes. Marin sat up. Sweat was pouring off of her now and she was glad for the cold cloth. Mom took the cloth, rinsed it and put it back on her head.

"Marin, do you feel better? Do you know where you are now?" she asked hoping for a correct answer.

Marin nodded her head. It was starting to ache even more. "My head hurts, but I'm okay. I know where I am."

"Well, why don't you relax a bit okay?" Dad replied with a worried look. "It must be stress. Did you have a bad dream?"

Marin wasn't sure how to answer that, so instead she shook her head yes. She didn't want them to think she was crazy or something. They had problems enough, with Josh and the little boys still missing.

Marin must have dozed off again because when she awoke, there was a ruckus going on outside. It sounded like the entire campground was outside trying to get in to the camper. Marin peered out of her sleeping area. No one was inside. Mom and Dad must be out. Jumping down, she grabbed her clothes and entered the closet size bathroom so she could change. Stepping outside, flash bulbs greeted her in the face along with camera crews and news reporters. Oh no, not again, she thought. How did they get wind of this anyway? Who would have told them? She couldn't think, because three reporters were trying to interview her at the same time and had shoved their microphones in her face.

"No comment," her dad said rescuing her before she uttered a word, leading her to their picnic table. Sitting there was mom, and Josh! When Marin saw him, she ran at him and almost tackled him with a flying hug.

"Why didn't you guys wake me up? Josh are you okay?" Josh nodded, his face beaming with happiness.

"We wanted to let you sleep some more after the incident this morning Marin. Besides, Josh just got here. That's why there are all of these reporters here trying to get interviews," Mom answered. "Although I think there are twice as many at Jessie's campsite. Her brothers were found this morning too."

"Oh, yes!" she exclaimed, hugging her brother again. Embarrassed now, Josh shrugged her off of himself.

"I didn't do anything," he said with a wink in Marin's direction. Marin looked at him with one eyebrow lifted. She wasn't sure what he meant, but she could plainly see that he was elated about something.

"The Park Rangers found the boys and Josh found a group of people that were out camping. The group had a satellite phone and called the Park Rangers. The Park Rangers met up with them and brought them all back here together."

"Are they okay?" she asked.

"The boys were a bit dehydrated and hungry, but otherwise okay," Mom answered. "And here is the weird part. They claim a huge dog found them, gave them food and water, then led them to the search team."

"Of course the dog conveniently disappeared," Dad added. "No one from the search team saw it. But the rescue team did say the blood hounds were barking and howling excessively at the time. They just attributed that to them picking up the scent of the boys, not the phantom dog."

Marin stood with her mouth open, realization dawning on her. A large dog found them? Marin stared at Josh's face hoping for clues as to what really happened out there. His face was unreadable, but his eyes were twinkling.

"Your mom and I have decided to cut our vacation short one day. I don't think we can handle any more adventures for a while," Dad said. Both kids looked heartbroken, but a bit relieved at the same time.

This had been a great vacation but Marin had a vicious headache from the stress of the last day. It would be great to be back home, Josh thought.

Back with my TV and video games and my friends. "When do we leave Dad?" he asked.

"We leave in an hour or so, so let's get packed up," And with that announcement, the whole family pushed past the two remaining reporters who had been standing nearby, and got themselves ready for the long trek back home.

Chapter 9

The trip back to Florida was restful. Josh slept most of the ride back, while Marin busied herself with reading. Marin was dying to know the details of what had happened to Josh in the woods that day, but she never got the chance to ask him. The camper was too small and they would be overheard by their parents. Marin didn't want to risk it, so she had to wait.

When they finally reached the house, they unloaded their stuff so dad could return the camper first thing in the morning.

Josh and Marin brought their laundry downstairs to sort it. The bus would be picking them up on Monday morning to take them to swim camp for three weeks, so they had to do laundry and pack again. All they really needed was a ton of swim suits, shorts, and lots of sun screen, Marin thought as she started the washer.

Marin was happy that she had an extra day home before they left again. She wanted to see Amy and Jill if she could before they left, and she was sure that Josh wanted to see his friends as well. Maybe we can order pizza and have a little party, she thought. That would be cool.

When both their parents were downstairs watching TV in the family room, Marin got her chance to talk to Josh about what had happened at the park. Tiptoeing to his door, she knocked lightly. "Josh, open up," she whispered.

Josh opened his door as quietly as he could and stood in the doorway listening. When he was sure they couldn't be overheard, he started to tell Marin his tale of changing into a wolf and finding the boys.

"I knew it," she answered simply when he was finished, smiling at him. "And I think you're gonna be amazed by how I knew."

"How did you know?"

"The morning you changed, I had a dream about being a wolf... a dream that didn't stop when I woke up, and was so disorienting that I didn't know where I was."

"You dreamt about me as a wolf?"

"Not dreamt about you, I was with you, inside your head sorta. It's kinda hard to explain,"

Marin added, a bit frustrated. "I was in the camper in my bed, but I was also running with you, seeing what you saw, hearing what you heard, and get this, smelling what you smelled. I smelled the campfire you found, I heard the blood hounds barking and howling, almost everything. I never saw you with the boys though."

It was now Josh's turn to stand there with his mouth open, staring at this sister while he tried to absorb everything Marin had just told him. With a sudden jolt he exclaimed, "You couldn't read my thoughts, could you?"

"No, thank goodness. I'm afraid that I might have to be locked up in a looney bin if I did." She added teasing. "But it was so eerie, and it gave me a horrible headache when it finally stopped."

"Aren't we two a pair though? Geez."

"Marin, Josh, come downstairs if you are still up!" Dad called upstairs to them. Startled, they both jumped a bit, afraid that they might have been overheard.

"What is it Dad?" Josh asked when they got downstairs.

"We have some bad news for you guys. Your mom and I were finishing up opening the mail and we found this," he said holding out an official looking letter. "It's from the director of your swim camp. They filed for bankruptcy and shut down their business two weeks ago. We will have to petition the bankruptcy court to get the money back that we paid them, if we can."

"So, we are pretty much screwed," Josh answered.

"Hey, watch your mouth young man," Mom replied.

"Oops, sorry Mom," Josh quickly added ducking his head while trying to look apologetic.

"So, what do we do now Dad?" Marin asked expectantly looking from one parent to the other.

"Well, for one thing, your mom still has her tutoring job for the rest of this summer. That means you guys are going to be on your own all day again. We think the best thing to do is to continue your plans for swimming. Since we can't afford to send you to another camp without getting the refund first, even if we could find one with availability, the best thing is for you guys to head to the public pool every day like you were doing before vacation. You would be swimming at camp every day anyway, so now you will be swimming here instead," Dad replied.

"I'll make a call to see if any of your regular instructors are available for the next few weeks before school starts again. If I can't get one or both of them, then you guys will have to go it alone and practice without one."

"Your mom is also going to be giving you both reading and short assignments to keep you busy during the day, plus chores, in an effort to keep the video games to a minimum," he said turning his head to look knowingly at Josh.

Josh wanted to reply back to his dad that he wouldn't waste the whole day playing video games, but he knew better. "Aw, man, this really bites...I mean this is terrible," Josh corrected himself changing the subject. "I was looking forward to seeing my friends there, so was Marin." Marin nodded her head in agreement, disappointment all over her face too.

"I know, but there isn't anything anyone can do at this point. Bankruptcy cases have to go through the court system. It may be months and months before we get the refund, if we get anything back at all. We have to deal with this now. Maybe next summer, you can meet up with your friends at a new camp," Mom replied. "They are in the same situation we are at the moment."

"Too bad they don't live close by," Marin added wishfully. "Then we wouldn't need camp. We could all just go to the pool every day."

"Well that would save us money, but your mom and I were hoping for more supervision, plus instruction."

"Hey Mom and Dad," Josh asked. "Can we go to the pool with our friends here?"

"I don't see why not," Mom replied while Dad nodded in agreement.

"Great!" Josh said, bouncing a bit up and down. "I'm going to call Danny right now."

"And I'm going to call Amy and Jill," Marin added.

"Okay, you two, go to bed now. I'll have your assignments for you in the morning."

"Aww, Ma, do we really have to have homework over the summer?" Josh whined.

"Hey, at least it won't be graded, right mom?" Marin said.

"No, guys, nothing is going to be graded," Mom chuckled. Just make sure they are completed, all right?"

"Okay mom. Good night," Josh replied, bolting up the stairs to make his phone call.

"Good night," Marin said as she kissed her parents good night and went upstairs as well. She had calls to make too.

****

Marin and Josh were excited the next morning. Even though Mom had left them both reading and math assignments to do before they went to go swimming, they were looking forward to fun days ahead with their friends at the pool. They didn't really get to hang out that much with their friends as much as they would have liked during the school year, especially when it was swimming season. Marin and Josh each had to get up early and head over to pool at the high school before classes. The middle school was allowed to use it before classes, while the high school students used it after classes.

Then there were swim meets at other schools after classes. And with the traveling involved getting to and from those meets, sometimes Josh and Marin didn't get home until late at night. Homework sometimes had to be done on the bus.

But this was going to be a treat. Hanging out with friends, plus swimming at the pool for the next few weeks, it didn't get any better than that, Josh thought to himself as he started on the day's assignments.

The plan was to be finished right around lunch time, eat lunch, then bike over to the pool with their friends. The pool was a bit of a distance away, but they didn't care. They decided against taking the bus like they did before they left for vacation. And the best part is that they could race each other if they wanted to while they were there. It's not like they would be racing in the ocean, as that was obviously dangerous. This was a huge public pool complete with refreshment stands and tables with umbrellas. Plus it had a section for little kids, lanes for doing laps and/or racing, two water slides, an area for water volleyball, and a huge area in the pool for just hanging and splashing about.

Of course the primary goal was to do laps and increase their speed for swim meets, as if they were at swim camp. And while they would miss their swim camp friends, at least they could hang out with their other friends for most of the day.

When they were ready to leave, Marin checked to make sure that she had plenty of sunscreen with her. She couldn't afford to get sunburned with her fair skin. Packing up her back pack, she added two towels, plus snacks for her and her brother. They would buy drinks once they got there, the pack would just be too heavy with those added, especially on a bike. And they hadn't had the time yet to replace the back pack that Josh gave the boys in the woods.

They all converged on Marin and Josh's house for the ride over at 1:30 pm. Josh was exhilarated at the thought of being able to spend his afternoons at the pool for the rest of the summer with his friends. He hoped to be able to run into other kids he knew as well.

It took them about a half an hour to get there, and as expected the place was overflowing with people. Once inside, the boys and the girls

145

went their separate ways. Josh and Danny headed over to the water slide, while Marin and her friends went to find chairs with umbrellas. Just because they had to arrive and depart together didn't mean they had to hang out while they were there. Marin and Josh had agreed on that in the morning while working on their assignments. They did decide to meet up and have a few races throughout the day though, just because they could.

"When are you guys going to race, huh Marin?" Jill asked as soon as they were seated in their chairs. "I'll be the referee," she volunteered with a big smile on her face.

"Okay, time to come clean Jill," Marin said with a big grin on her face as well. "Do you have a thing for my brother or what?"

Jill kept smiling and slowly nodded her head. "I knew it," Marin gloated. "I knew it last month when you were over helping us with my room, and at the painting party. I knew I had never seen you so quiet," Marin laughed.

"Hey," Jill answered, trying to sound a bit outraged. "That's not funny. Oh all right, maybe it is," she said when she saw Amy smirking as well. "Hey, we can't help who we like, can we?"

"No, we can't," Amy answered for her. "I guess we're just slaves to our raging teenage hormones!" All three of them burst out laughing so loudly that the people in the surrounding chairs turned to stare at them.

"Well, I have some bad news for you."

"What?" Jill asked, a look of worry crossing her face.

"Josh met someone at the campground last week. He thinks he's in love," Marin said with her best theatrical voice, exaggerating the word love. This caused Amy to burst out laughing again.

"I'm glad you think it's funny," Jill said, clearly not amused.

"How long can it last?" Marin added. "She lives in Maryland. We'll probably never see her again."

"Besides Jill, you have the home team advantage!" Amy added enthusiastically. "You have us!"

"Yeah you do! So, don't worry. It shouldn't last too long," Marin added cheerfully. "I'm sure he'll be over her quick."

Meanwhile on the other side of the pool, Danny and Josh were going on the waterslide nonstop. Once they got off, they trekked to the back of the line to wait for another turn. Danny was practically bouncing like Josh usually did, which was unlike him.

"What's wrong with you today Danny? I don't think I've ever seen you like this."

"I don't really know Josh. I guess I'm just in a great mood today." Pausing a few seconds, he added, "Um, when we are done here, do you wanna go sit by your sister and her friends?"

"Not really. Marin and I thought we should give each other some room, you know what I mean? Some space. We just spent a week together in that small camper. I think we're sick of each other at the moment," he added jokingly. "Besides, I have to tell you what happened while we were away. I couldn't risk saying anything in front of Jill."

"What happened?" Danny asked getting all serious. "Did Marin change again?"

"Well," Josh said pulling Danny aside and out of the line, "No, not Marin. Me. I can do what she does. I can change into an animal too."

"What? You mean we've been here for almost an hour already and you didn't bother to tell me until now?" Danny asked incredulously. "So, what happened? How did it go? I guess no one saw you or we probably wouldn't be having this conversation."

Josh spent the next ten minutes or so telling Danny the whole story. He omitted the part where Marin was inside his head though. He wasn't sure why, it was still just too creepy to talk about, even to his best friend. All the time that Josh spoke, Danny just stood there with his mouth open, not saying anything.

"I don't know Josh," Danny finally replied. "You and Marin have a very special gift. I don't know how long you will be able to keep it a secret from the rest of the world."

"Tell me about it, reporters showed up again at the campsite. That's two times in less than two months that's happened. And you know, I swear one of them looked like a reporter from Jacksonville who tried to interview Marin after she disappeared in the ocean."

"I really don't know how it could be the same reporter. How did they get up there from Jax anyway? But you do have a point; first Marin went missing, then you. It does seem to be a pattern," he mused.

"I don't see how they could. We each went missing trying to save someone else. It's not like we decided to just pick up and go," he added. "I do feel good about what I did, and would gladly do it again. Helping people is fun. And boy was it a rush when I changed. I don't know how to describe it."

"I supposed it helped that there was a pretty girl you were trying to impress," he teased. "And speaking of girls, when is your first race with Marin?" he asked, changing the subject back.

Josh looked at him and gave him a huge smile, grinning from ear to ear. "Uh oh, not you too," he said covering his eyes and not looking at his friend. "Which one is it? Jill or Amy? And please, please I beg you, don't say Marin."

Danny hesitated for a few seconds trying to decide if he should tell him. "Jill," he finally answered in a whisper.

"Oh thank goodness. I don't know if I could have handled it if you said Marin. But I do know how you feel at least," Josh said shaking his head. "At least Jill lives near us, Jessie lives in a whole other state. We've been texting and chatting online, but it's not the same thing. And, who knows when I'll be able to see her again? But as far as the racing is concerned, we talked about the first one to happen around 3:30 or so."

"It's almost that time now," Danny replied eagerly. "Should we go get them?"

****

"On your mark, get set, go!" Jill yelled.

Josh and Marin both kicked off from the side of the pool creating a huge splash, as diving was forbidden in this area of the pool. Marin quickly took the lead with Josh keeping pace only one stroke behind her. This race was to the far side of the pool and back using the backstroke. The next race would use the crawl, and the third race would use the butterfly stroke, with breaks in between races. The winner of two out of three races would be declared the winner for the day, and have to do the others chores the next day.

Marin kept up the lead and won, but just barely. Pulling themselves out of the pool, they were greeted by Jill, whose face had gone white.

"Jill, what is it?" Marin asked as Amy handed her a towel.

"My dad just called," she said as tears started to slowly build up and trickle from her eyes. "My brother disappeared."

"Oh, my gosh, what happened?" Danny asked.

"My dad got home late last night from work. You know we have an aide that helps out? Well, the aide asked to go home early cause he wasn't feeling well and dad said yes. My dad fell asleep on the couch and when he woke up, my brother was gone. He found the front door open."

"Did he call the police yet?" Amy asked.

"Yes, it was the first call he made," Jill answered, tears now flowing freely down her cheeks.

"Come on guys, we have to leave," Josh replied looking at the four of them. "Pack up quickly, I have an idea."

"But what can we do?" Jill asked as they grabbed their stuff and got ready to leave. "I guess we could search for him on our bikes, but then what? How can we possibly find Aaron? He could be anywhere. He's been wandering for at least two hours according to my dad."

Leaving the pool, the five of them rode faster than they thought possible back to Marin's and Josh's house, passing by Jill's house to look at the spectacle. They saw the police swarming over the place like bees, as well as the local News crews. Oh crap, Josh thought. Not again.

"Why did we go to your house Josh?" Jill asked when they stopped. "I should be home, with my dad."

"Like I said at the pool Jill, I have an idea. Marin and I have a secret we need to tell you. It's a big one. Can we trust you with it? I thought of a way to find Aaron, but we need to move quickly."

"Josh, you're not thinking what I think you are thinking... are you?" Marin asked. "You really want to tell Jill? I'm sorry Jill," she quickly added when she saw the look on her face. "But it's a life changing secret and we need to be able to trust you. Can you keep it?" Marin implored with a twinge of hesitation.

"What new secret Marin?" Amy asked. "Is there something new I don't know about?"

"Yes there is Amy. I'm sorry, but I haven't had a chance to tell you about Josh. He can do it too." Amy gave Marin a startled look, but didn't say anything.

"Can do what?" Jill snapped, her patience running out.

Josh looked at her. "You have to promise first," he replied.

"Okay, I solemnly swear to keep this big secret. Please, how can you guys help us find Aaron?" she answered, her voice starting to crack.

"Josh and I can change into animals," Marin replied simply. "I changed into a dolphin to save Josh that day at the beach, and I changed into a dog the following month." Marin purposely left out the part where she said she'd wanted to bite Josh.

"And I changed into a wolf just last week to find two little boys who were lost in the woods," Josh added.

Jill turned to look at Amy and Danny. "You guys believe them?" she asked.

"I saw Marin change into the dog," Danny replied looking her in the eyes and taking her hand in his. "It's true, every word of it." Gently using her hand, he crossed his heart.

Jill promptly sat down, trying her best to believe them. Danny sat down next to her in an effort to comfort her.

"I was at the beach Jill," Amy added as well. "I saw Marin dive down and a dolphin come up. And I believe my best friend." Amy looked up at Marin and gave Jill a pat on the back.

"So, what's the plan Josh?" Danny asked. "What are you going to do?"

"Well, I think our best bet is to change into dogs," Josh replied. "We can hunt Aaron down by smell. I think people would freak out if they saw wolves."

"I don't know. Won't the police be using dogs? What if someone tries to catch you?" Jill asked, still a bit skeptical.

"I've got an idea, how about coyotes? They are faster than dogs, but have the same characteristics, such as a great nose for smelling and excellent hearing. And they hunt in twos," Amy added. "They're also smaller and I think would be harder to catch."

"How do you know all this?" Marin asked.

"I saw it on TV last week. They've been spotted in this part of Florida."

"What does everyone think? Coyotes, dogs, or wolves? You don't think people would be freaked out seeing coyotes running around?" Josh asked the group.

"I think we should try coyotes." Turning to Jill, Marin said, "I guess we probably need something of Aaron's to smell."

"I hope we can do it. We've never purposely tried to change before. It usually happens when we're angry or frustrated," Josh mused.

"Or really ticked off at someone," Marin finished for him with a smirk on her face.

Danny stood up at this and pulled Jill up with him. "I'll go with Jill back to her house. She needs to get home. She can sneak me out something of Aaron's to bring back here for you guys to get a fix on."

"Good luck," was all Jill could muster up, her eyes pleading. Danny led her outside to get their bikes.

"See you in a bit," Danny said to them on his way out.

"So guys, how are you going to do this?" Amy asked. She was nervous as she hadn't seen Marin change yet and no one had ever seen Josh change.

"I don't know," Marin answered. "Josh seems to think we should be able to change just by thinking about it. Tell ya the truth, it has me a bit scared thinking about changing on purpose."

"Well, I don't see why. Here's the deal. When I was in the woods, I was frustrated, but I don't think I was as crazy as you were that day in the attic. I don't think we need to be nuts or anything. We can just focus and concentrate on it. We have to try it at least."

157

"But wait," Amy interrupted. "So, unlike the first time Marin changed, Josh you remembered everything that happened didn't you?"

"Yep. I did. All of it. From the get go."

"Cool."

"Okay, I got an idea. I'll go get my laptop and we can find pics of coyotes to help us focus. How about that?" Marin asked.

"Why not? We need to wait for Danny though."

Marin ran upstairs and brought her laptop down and put it on the kitchen table. "Should we try to change in here or go outside?"

"In here. We can't take the chance that someone could see us."

While they waited for Danny to come back, Marin found a website with a large photo of a coyote for them to concentrate on.

"Okay, I hate to bring up an obvious point here guys, but what do you intend to do once you find Aaron? Assuming of course, that you do find him." Amy asked, ever practical.

"Well, I was thinking about that too. I guess if we find him, we wait and follow him around until we change back," Marin answered.

"We'll do our best to keep an eye on him. I don't know if we could lead him anywhere, but at least we can try to protect him," Josh added.

Ten minutes later Danny knocked on the front door and let himself in. "Here," he said holding out one of Aaron's shirts. "Are you guys ready?"

"I guess we'll see!" Josh replied with enthusiasm. As much as it hurt him to see Jill so upset, he was excited to have a mission again. He so wanted to feel the exhilaration that he felt in the forest that day while he was running. It was starting to make him a little antsy.

Marin noticed that Josh was starting to get jittery as well. That might help, she thought. "We need to think about poor Jill and her Dad and how they must be feeling at the moment. If we can channel their stress, we shouldn't have a problem changing." Josh nodded his head at this. Both kids stared intently at the picture of the coyote and closed their eyes.

Within seconds they dropped to the floor and began the swift change into coyotes, the fur rippling outward from their backs down to their feet. Amy gawked at them, her mouth wide open. Taking a step back, she grabbed onto Danny for support and gasped when she met the eyes of two coyotes, one with big blue eyes. Keeping a tight hold of Amy, Danny leaned forward and put Aaron's shirt in front of both of their noses so they could get a good sniff.

Inhaling deeply, coyote-Marin and Josh turned and trotted toward the door while Danny held it open for them. Moving in single file, they slunk into the bushes near the side of the house and were gone without a sound.

Danny turned to look at Amy. Her eyes were still wide and she hadn't spoken yet. "It gets easier to watch the more you see it happen," he joked trying to ease her tension. Amy smiled at this, staring off in the direction they'd gone. A moment later the front door opened and Marin's and Josh's mom walked in. All three jumped.

Mom looked from Amy to Danny, her eyebrows shooting up in confusion. Amy broke from her trance and spoke quickly, trying to cover for her friends. "Um, they just left. Marin lost her cell phone on the way back from the pool and they went to find it. We said we'd leave you a note and would go and help look too."

"Okay," Mom answered, with a bit of hesitation in her voice, not really believing this. "Why didn't Josh call me from his phone or from the house?"

"I don't know," he shrugged. "They ran out of here too fast to think about it?" Danny added grasping at what he thought might be a reasonable explanation. "Besides, his phone is there on the table," he added pointing to it sitting next to Marin's laptop. Reaching over, he swiftly closed it, hiding the image of the coyote they had been looking at.

"We're going to go help them look," Danny said as he grabbed Amy by the arm and escorted her out the front door.

"Hey, can one of you call me when you catch up to them?" Mom asked as they closed the door behind them "Okay, Mrs. Royce!" Amy answered.

"Call her, how can you call her?" Danny asked when they were on their bikes. "What could we possibly tell her?"

"What was I supposed to say? Sorry, Mrs. R., but your kids are searching Jacksonville as coyotes looking for a little lost boy? I'll let you know when they find him? Besides, I'm a kid. I can always say I forgot to call. Correct me if I'm wrong, but kids aren't too reliable."

"What if she calls you?"

"I can just say my phone died. Works every time as long as you don't overuse it. I just hope she doesn't call my house. That might be a problem."

****

Coyote-Marin and Josh stopped in the bushes of the next door neighbor's house and both lifted their noses into the wind. Within seconds they took off running with Josh in front, keeping as close to houses and parked cars as physically possible to avoid being seen. *This isn't like the last time*, Coyote-Josh thought to himself.

What about the last time? Coyote-Marin answered back, her voice inside his head. Coyote-Josh jammed on his brakes and came to an abrupt stop causing Coyote-Marin to crash into him. The impact sent Coyote-Marin and Josh somersaulting over each other. They both wound up sprawled under a huge rose bush. *Oww! Man that hurt. Look at me! I'm all scratched. What'd you do that for?* Coyote-Marin got up slowly and carefully maneuvered her way out from under the bush, trying not to get any more scratches.

What did you say? Shaking his head back and forth in a futile attempt to dislodge what he was hearing from his brain, he carefully made his way out from under the rose bush.

I said, what about last time? Coyote-Marin looked directly into Coyote-Josh's eyes when she did this, hoping not to freak him out again. *I thought this might happen,* she told him in his mind, changing the subject.

What, what did you think might happen? Coyote-Josh answered still agitated.

I had the feeling that we might be able to talk with our minds if we were both changed into animals. Remember what happened at the park? You were a wolf, but it was like I was there too, running with you in the woods. I could see what you saw as if I was right there with you.

Well when the heck were you going to tell me? He growled and glared at her, stamping his paws in agitation.

I wasn't sure it would happen, she thought, looking at him with her big blue eyes. *It was just a guess, a theory I had until now.*

Marin, next time, would you please tell me, preferably in advance? You know I hate surprises. Geez! Come on, let's go find Aaron now okay? We don't have a lot of time. I think he went this way.

Coyote-Josh once again lifted his snout into the air and inhaled deeply. The wind had picked up a bit he noticed. Looking up at the sky, he noticed thunderclouds off in the distance. *Great, just great. What else can go wrong now? Just what we need, a quick afternoon thunderstorm. That'll wash away every scent Aaron left.* Turning himself around, he led them on a fast run in the direction of Aaron, or at least he hoped he did.

I hope we can find him before the rain starts, Marin agreed, keeping perfect pace with her brother as they ran side by side.

They approached Jill's house as stealthily as possible, looking to verify the trail that Aaron left. There were so many police cars and camera crews around that wanted to minimize the risk of being seen, if at all possible. They wound up two houses away, sniffing the ground.

What's this wonderful smell, Coyote-Marin thought. *Josh, can you tell what it is? Part of it is Aaron's scent, but I don't know what the other one is, do you?* Both Coyote- Marin and Josh had picked up Aaron's faint trail, but it was overlaid with another stronger irresistible odor. Josh sniffed where Marin had, and looked up at her with drool dripping from his mouth.

I don't know, Coyote-Josh thought. *I didn't run across this scent when I was a wolf. Come on, let's keep following it… I mean them…. I mean Aaron.*

What's the matter with you! Coyote-Marin thought. *Why are you drooling like that? Are you okay?*

Yes, darn it. I'm okay. I don't know why my mouth is doing this. I just sniffed that spot and now I'm drooling. I can't help it. It's just a little drool.

Coyote-Josh looked at Coyote-Marin and did his best shrug, for a coyote that is. *We're coyotes. I guess we are going to react to things like this whether we want to or not. Ummm... It kinda happened before to me when I was in the woods.*

What do you mean happened before? Coyote Marin thought. *Is there something you forgot to tell me?*

Yeah. I chased a rabbit. I couldn't help myself. I was hungry. It was there and I tried to get it.

You didn't though, did you? She thought, horrified.

No, it got away.

Great, Coyote-Marin thought, *just great. This could wind up being a big problem if we can't control ourselves better.*

I know. I'll try to be more focused.

I sure hope so, Coyote-Marin thought, trying not to be worried.

Hey, I heard that, Coyote-Josh thought.

This is so annoying, you being in my head, Coyote-Marin thought as they made off in the direction of the new scent and Aaron.

How much time do you think we've been like this? Coyote-Josh thought.

I don't know. It's not like I have a watch on or my cell with me, Coyote-Marin replied sarcastically. They had been on Aaron's trail for what felt like hours, but in reality it had probably been about twenty minutes. *Do you feel a change in the air? It's like the air is charged or something.*

Yeah, I feel it.... Coyote-Josh answered her while sniffing the ground, his ears pulled back on the side of his head, simultaneously listening. *Looks like the rain and thunderstorm are going to be here quicker than we thought.*

They found themselves on the outskirts of the suburb they lived in standing before an undeveloped wooded area. *Why don't I recognize this place? Have you ever seen this before?* Coyote-Josh asked.

No, I didn't know there were any kinds of woods near our house. Well, not too near. We've been moving at a good clip for a while. I have no idea how far we've come. Do you still pick up his scent?

Yeah, it leads into these woods.

Uh, oh! Crap! Coyote-Marin heard it just as Coyote-Josh did. Snap, went a twig and then the howling and barking began. *Run Josh! Run! Coyote-Marin yelled in his head. Police and their dogs! They've spotted us, run!*

Coyote-Josh glanced quickly over his shoulder and met the gaze of two police officers with their tracking dogs headed their way, guns out. The dogs were snarling, barking and literally foaming at the mouth in their efforts to reach them.

Crack! Crack! Crack! *What the? Are they shooting at us?* Coyote-Marin screamed in his head. *Why're they shooting at us? What did we do? We're coyotes, not wolves!*

Run, split up! Coyote-Josh cried. *Run in a zig zag! Don't give them a target!*

Crack, crack, crack! The gun went off three more times in their direction. Coyote-Josh and Coyote-Marin split up each racing off in an opposite direction, running in a zig zag to avoid the bullets landing near them. Coyote-Marin reached cover first, finding refuge in the safety of some bushes at the entrance to the woods. Josh did his best to disappear behind some huge trees, keeping as low as he could while still running.

****

Danny and Amy didn't know where they were headed but they thought they would patrol the neighborhood looking for a glimpse of Marin and Josh. After twenty minutes of searching, they decided to call it quits. They needed to get home, as it was already past dinner time.

"How about we go and check on Jill and see how she's doing?" Danny asked. He needed to get home, his mom had texted him twice already. He didn't know how long he could put her off, but he was feeling a bit guilty over having left Jill.

"I don't think that's a good idea. I'm sure the place is still crawling with police and news crews. Do you think they'll let you in to see her?"

"I don't see why not. We're her friends after all. It's not like we had anything to do with Aaron's disappearance."

"I tell you what, let's ride by the house and see what's going on. Your mom is going to kill you if you don't get home, and so is mine. If they let us in, great. We can call them from her house and let them know where we are. And if not..."

Amy and Danny approached Jill's house with caution. Police cars and news crews with their vans were still parked up and down the block. They now had the section of road blocked off in front of Jill's house with yellow tape.

Getting off their bikes, they approached the tape. They were about to scoot under it, when they were stopped by a police officer hurrying toward them waving his hands.

"No one is allowed in to see the family at this time," he said.

"But Jill is our friend," Danny answered with a determined look on his face.

"Only close relatives are allowed in and we have to verify it."

Amy shook her head at Danny and looked glum. There was no way to get around that. "Time to go home. Call me later if you hear anything, okay?"

****

Coyote-Marin felt drained. *How long have we been out here? It feels like I've been running* around for days. In her effort to avoid the police and their dogs, she had lost Aaron's scent. And she'd lost Josh. *Josh, can you hear me?* Coyote-Marin thought, squinting her eyes closed.

Where are you? Nothing, no reply came from Josh inside her head. *Great. Just great. Crap! What should I do? Should I keep looking or just go home? This sucks*, she thought.

Oh!! I got an idea! Lifting her head into the wind, she took a deep breath and let out her best coyote howl.

It took ten seconds for another coyote to answer her with its howl. *Geez, I hope that was Josh*, she thought. *What did Amy say about coyotes being in Florida? I guess I'll wait and see if he shows up.*

Coyote-Marin didn't have to wait long. Another coyote did appear, but it wasn't Josh. The fur on her body instinctively stood on end, forming a peak down the center of her back. As it crept into her view, it kept its head down, its eyes unblinking.

Now what do I do? Coyote-Marin thought as she turned and fled at top speed away from the real coyote. *JOSH!! Where are you!!*

Over here! Coyote-Josh answered her at last when she came charging around an abandoned car straight at him. *Stop! He said into her thoughts. I found Aaron!*

There's a real coyote behind me! Coyote-Marin yelled into his head as she ducked behind the car and crawled on the ground to hide under it. *I don't know if I lost it or not. It found me when I let out a howl looking for you, so I ran.* Coyote- Marin was panting hard and trembling. She had never been so scared in her life.

Coyote-Josh pricked up his ears and lifted his face once again into the wind to take a deep breath. He was listening and seeing if he could smell the other coyote. *I don't hear or smell it Marin,* he thought. *Maybe it was as scared of you as you were of it?*

I don't know about that, she thought climbing out to stand next to him. She was still shaking a little.

Relax, Coyote-Josh thought. *Maybe it just wanted to be friends. It's just us here right now. Aaron is inside the car. And I figured out what the intriguing smell is. It's a momma cat and her kittens.* Coyote-Marin jumped up and placed her two paws on the car to see inside the vehicle. There was Aaron, sitting with a cat and her kittens in the back seat of the decrepit car.

I did three laps around this thing to see if there is a way in or out for us. There isn't. The momma cat can get in and out but I have no idea how Aaron got in. The car looks rusty and I haven't seen him try to open a door. Maybe he isn't capable of it. I don't know. But at least we found him. That's a bonus, he thought continuing to circle the car.

With that, the sky opened up, the torrential rain drenching them both in seconds. *Great, just great,* Coyote-Marin thought. *Just what we need. So, what do we do now? Should we wait until we change back? We didn't bring a cell phone or anything...how do we tell people about Aaron? Or should we try and get a cop's attention again and lead them here?*

I don't like that last option Marin... do you WANT to be shot at again? I think my biggest problem is that I really, really wanna eat that cat. And with that drool began oozing out of his mouth again.

Josh, are you crazy!!! Get a grip on yourself. We're here to help, geez what's wrong with you! Coyote-Marin wanted to smack him, but of course she couldn't because she didn't have any hands. What she did have though, was small sharp teeth. Reaching over she bit him on his shoulder.

Owww! Cut it out! I told you this scent is driving me crazy. I'm trying to control myself...I really am. I swear! Coyote-Josh thought while pacing back and forth. *We need to think this through a little better the next time. If I didn't already regret changing into a coyote when we were being shot at, this is now the icing on the cake.*

How do you think I feel? That real coyote scared the heck out of me. Maybe he just wanted to form a pack, but wow. We totally screwed this up. We have no way to get Aaron out of the vehicle and no way to tell anyone he's here. We're in way over our heads. We really need to think more carefully about what kind of animal we change into.

The rain was still coming down in buckets and with the addition of thunder and lightning, Josh was thankful that they were able to read each other minds. They would have had to yell to be heard with what the weather was throwing at them. Josh thought, *we just need to wait it out till we change back. The police dogs won't be able to track anything now; the rain will have washed Aaron's scent away.*

Let's get some cover, Coyote-Marin said as she crawled back under the car, hoping for some shelter from the storm. She felt the car moving a bit due to Aaron rocking back and forth, singing something.

Yeah, one second, Coyote-Josh answered. *I gotta take care of business.* Walking around the nearest tree, he lifted his leg.

What are you doing? Coyote-Marin said into his head. *Are your brains falling out of your head? Did you just take a leak in front of me?*

Sorry, but I've been holding it forever.

You're killing me Josh, she answered exasperated. *What is wrong with you? I mean, really?*

Coyote-Marin laid her head on her paws, trying to relax. She was willing herself to change back into human form. She was concentrating so hard, she never sensed the other coyote until its cold wet nose poked her in her side. *Ahhhhhh!* She yelled and quickly extracted herself from the car, barreling over Coyote-Josh in an effort to escape.

What the? Oh, no! The other coyote! Hold on Marin, he thought. *Maybe it wants to be friends. It didn't bite you, did it?*

No. But what do you think it wants? Coyote-Marin thought as she moved to stand behind him and peek over his shoulder at it.

Maybe the same thing I do, Coyote-Josh answered. *To eat the cat and her kittens,* he thought glumly. Coyote-Josh lowered his head and let out a growl. Encouraged by her brother and feeling a bit braver, Coyote-Marin stood next to him and did the same thing. Even though it was now two coyotes to one, the real coyote didn't back down.

Now what do we do? Coyote-Marin thought. *Do you think it wants to fight us for the cats? It can't be after Aaron, can it?*

I have no idea. Either way, it can't have Aaron or the cats. The real coyote started to snarl in reply to this, almost as if it could read their minds too. All three of them started to slowly circle around each other, with Coyote-Marin and Josh finally ending up with their backs up against the driver's side of the car almost as a form of a defensive position for Aaron and the cats.

The pelting rain was making it hard to see, but the thunder had stopped so they could still hear a little. Someone or something was crashing through the brush right toward them. All three coyotes turned as one when the bicycle and its rider emerged headed in their direction.

"Get away from them!" Danny shouted, as his bike skidded to a halt next to the car, stopping inches away from Coyote-Marin and Josh. The real coyote lit on out of there as if its tail was on fire.

"Marin and Josh, I can't believe I found you!" Danny exclaimed out of breath and exhilarated.

Coyote-Marin and Josh first looked at each other and then stared at Danny, their mouths hanging open in surprise. Coyote-Josh jumped up on the car, looked at Danny, and then looked inside the car, alternating looking at Danny and inside the car. Coyote Marin did the same thing. It only took Danny two seconds to figure out what they were trying to tell him. Whipping out his cell phone, he called his mom.

"Mom, I found Aaron!" he shouted into his phone. "He's locked in an abandoned car near grandma's house." It took a couple of minutes for Danny to do a better job of describing where they were to his mom so she could send the police to him.

In the meantime, Coyote-Marin and Josh were pacing. As soon as Danny hung up the phone, Coyote-Josh whined at him. "Yeah, you guys better go. You don't want anyone to see you change. My guess is that's it's been about an hour and a half since you went looking for Aaron. It could be anytime now."

Coyote-Marin and Josh barely waited for him to finish speaking before they lit off at a break neck pace back to their house as fast as their coyote legs could carry them. While tracking Aaron's scent had slowed them down, the run back to their house was exceptionally fast. They ran as if their lives depended on it, because in a way it did. They needed to be somewhere safe when the change back occurred.

Chapter 10

Creeping up on their house, they noticed the lights on and Mom's van in the driveway. Oh, no... Coyote-Marin thought. *What do we do now? How do we get in?* Coyote-Marin was about to reach full panic mode, her eyes searching the area for anyone who might see them. Coyote-Josh's eyes did the same thing, sweeping the area for somewhere safe they could change back. *That's it! The shed! Inside! Now! We can squeeze ourselves in!*

Pushing the rusted door with her all of her body weight, Coyote-Marin managed to widen the gap for Josh to get in. *Oww!* She cried. *I just got a splinter from that thing.* The door left a six-inch scrape on her right shoulder, complete with a bit of blood. *Geez! We have to get this door fixed,* Coyote-Josh thought as he wrangled himself in just in time. Within mere seconds of entering the shed, Marin and Josh resumed their human forms.

Marin and Josh stumbled into a standing position and grabbed each other's arms to steady themselves. There wasn't much room in the shed at the moment as one of their friends had thought to hide their bikes inside. Hard to pretend you're out looking for a lost cell phone on a bike if the bike you're supposed to be riding is still at home.

"Remind me to thank whoever hid our bikes," Josh said as he peeked out of the shed to see if any of their neighbors were around. "The coast is clear. Come on. Time to see how ticked off Mom is at us."

Marin and Josh grabbed the shed door and using all of their might, got it fully open so they could take out their bikes. The rain was just a light drizzle at the moment, but it didn't matter. They were already soaked to the skin. Jumping on their bikes, they pedaled up to the house. Josh slowly opened the garage door, trying not to alert their mom, but it was too late. The garage door made a screech as he grabbed the handle and yanked it up over his head.

Slam went the front door. In a few short strides Mom confronted them as they struggled to find a spot in the garage to store their bikes. "Where have you two been? You can't honestly tell me that you were out all of this time looking for Marin's cell phone!" Mom paced back and forth as she continued her tirade at them. "Over two hours! In the rain!" The anger in her voice made the words sound shrill. "Both of you! You're drenched and bleeding!" she added pointing at Marin's shoulder.

Mom stopped right in front of Josh and folded her arms. Her gaze was so intense that neither Josh nor Marin would dare look up at her. They knew better. She could spot a fib a mile away. Marin stole a quick side glance at her brother and took a deep breath to clear her head. Better tell her the truth. She would wheedle it out of them anyway. Josh could never stand up to her interrogation. Marin knew her brother too well, he would cave.

"Mom, we did go looking for my cell phone. But we also went looking for Aaron too." Josh gawked at this sister when she said this, but didn't say anything.

"Josh is that true?" Mom asked leaning over and lifting Josh's face so their eyes could meet.

"Yes," he whispered, letting out his breath. "We've been looking for Aaron almost the whole time."

Mom shook her head looking from kid to kid. "I can't believe the two of you have been gone this long, and no one thought to call me and tell me where you were and what you were doing," she exclaimed exasperated. Without hesitating she added, "You're both grounded. You two will spend the rest of the summer cleaning out this garage." And with that, she turned briskly and strode back into the house, slamming the door once again.

Chapter 11

The last remnants of summer swept by and were blissfully uneventful. Danny got all of the credit for finding Aaron and wound up on the front page of the newspaper. "Local Young Hero saves Autistic Boy!" read the headline with Danny's photo splashed across the paper. Marin chuckled when she saw the photo they were using of him. It was a few years old and it made Danny look even younger than Aaron. Anything to sell a story, Marin thought.

Thumbing through the paper Marin found a small blurb about two coyotes being spotted in the woods and the precautions they suggested you take with your pets. When Marin pointed this out to Josh, he just shrugged and said, "I told you so."

Mom was able to find Marin and Josh a temporary swim instructor to help them out during the day at the pool with their practices. Their mornings were spent cleaning out the garage, while their afternoons were spent at the pool, under supervision.

Marin was excited about how much better they were doing with their swimming.

"There's something to be said for being grounded," she said to Josh on their last afternoon of summer vacation as they packed up their gear and got ready to head home from the pool.

"Yeah, what's that?"

"How much better have our race times gotten in the last two weeks? I guess without anything else to focus on like friends...we can concentrate on getting better and faster in the water."

Josh thought about this for a moment, then he shrugged. "Yes, I guess. But I'm really missing my friends. Aren't you?"

"Sure am. I never thought we would be that excited for school to start again, even if it does mean homework."

"I feel like we've spent the whole summer grounded."

Getting on their bikes, they headed in the direction of home. Mom was done with her part time tutoring job so she'd be waiting for them. They had strict orders to be home by 4:30 pm or face dire consequences. Going without friends was bad enough, but not having TV or the internet would have been downright horrendous, so neither kid suggested any detour to possibly sneak in a quick visit with a friend.

"Hey, wanna race the rest of the way?" Josh yelled as they approached the loading dock and garbage area behind their nearby supermarket. "Let's start at the exit ramp!" He called again to Marin without waiting for her to answer.

Slowing slightly to round the corner of the building, they both came to a screeching halt when they almost collided with a pedestrian. The sudden effort of stopping locked up the brakes on Marin's bike and she flew over her handlebars into the adjacent grass next to two dumpsters. Josh jumped off his bike and ran to her side. "Are you okay?" he asked and sat down next to her to see.

Marin slowly sat up and pulled off her bike helmet. "Yeah, I think so," she said rubbing her knee. "Hmmmm, I'm bleeding," she added as an afterthought. Marin held up her hands for Josh to see the small trickle of blood that had formed on each palm.

"YOU!" yelled the pedestrian they had almost crashed into, pointing at Marin. "I've been waiting for this - all summer."

The color quickly drained from Marin's face. Grabbing Marin by the arm, Josh pulled her to her feet and folded his arms across his chest in an effort to look intimidating. Mimicking her brother, Marin crossed her arms too and stood her ground next to her brother, staring at the guy.

Peter Boyle closed the distance between them, his eyes twinkling with delight. "Really?" he laughed, placing his hands on his hips. "You two are gonna fight me? How about I stuff you both into those dumpsters?" he taunted, pointing at the dumpsters behind them. Peter Boyle had grown so tall over this past summer that he now stood a foot taller than them.

Marin stole a quick glance behind her at the dumpsters. Oh boy, this is it, she thought looking back at her nemesis. This is what I get for having a big mouth and losing my temper. He's gonna cream us and there isn't anything we can do about it. Almost as if she were replaying that day at school, an object flew over their heads from behind the dumpsters and landed with a thud.

This time it wasn't Peter doing the throwing; he'd been on the receiving end. A baseball hit him squarely on top of his head, the impact causing him to fall to his knees. Blood started to careen down his face.

Laughter echoed behind them. Marin and Josh ducked down so the new tormentors couldn't see them. Keeping low, they wedged themselves between the two dumpsters in an attempt to hide.

Seconds later, the boys who threw the ball emerged from around the side of the dumpsters. "Excellent aim Bruno! Now we know why you're our star pitcher. Stealing bikes now, dummy?" the apparent leader called out to Peter. "You aren't smart enough to do that!" The two other boys with him laughed at that and picked up Josh's and Marin's bikes to inspect them.

The leader approached Peter Boyle and stood silently. Without looking up, Peter reached into his pocket for his money and handed it up to the leader, keeping his eyes averted.

"Nice bikes," one of the others said to the

leader. "I know someone we can sell them to, though it won't let you off the hook for your weekly cash contribution."

All three boys laughed again.

Over my dead body, Marin thought, anger swelling up inside her. She tried to lunge, but she and Josh were wedged between the dumpsters and he easily blocked her. Grabbing her arms, he slowly shook his head, an eerie calm expression on his face considering the predicament they were in. Mouthing a word in an effort to remain undetected, he finally had to whisper it to Marin when she shook her head two times, not understanding what he was trying to say.

"Rottweilers?" He finally breathed into her ear. The gang of boys once again laughed at something they said to Peter.

Marin's big blue eyes went wide and she nodded, a broad smile spreading across her face. "But won't he see?" Marin whispered back. Peter Boyle was in clear view of them from his kneeling position in the grass. Josh shrugged and mouthed, I don't care.

Instantly making up her mind, Marin dropped to her knees first, arching her back as the change exploded all over her body, fur rippling out in a silent wave. Josh dropped down a second after her, their swift change into Rottweilers completed. They emerged from between the dumpster's softly growling, teeth bared, the golden brown fur bristling down the length of their backs for added intimidation.

Peter Boyle's tormentors turned to them and froze. All of the fun they'd been having at his expense wiped clean from their faces, now replaced by stone cold fear. Rottie-Marin and Rottie-Josh approached menacingly, their growls getting louder with each step closer. Almost as if in a dance, with each step they took closer, the three tormentors moved step for step to the other side of Peter Boyle, placing him in between them and the snarling dogs.

"You're late!" Peter Boyle exclaimed, startling the three boys who jumped in response. "Say hello to my new friends?" he added, sweeping his hands in a broad arc in the air from the direction of the dogs, to the direction of his tormentors, who were still backing up. "Sic em?" he asked almost begging, and looked directly into Rottie- Marin's blue eyes, as she and Josh were now standing next to him in the grass.

Chase and bark, but no biting, Rottie-Josh thought.

Oh all right, Rottie-Marin answered inside his head. *But I really want to bite these jerks.*

Both dogs sprang up and leapt at the tormentors, who responded by shrieking and sprinting away. Of course, they were no match for Rottweilers. Keeping a close distance from their teeth, Rottie-Marin and Rottie-Josh chased those boys for three blocks; snapping and barking at them all the way.

Well, that was fun! Rottie Josh thought. *I think they learned their lesson. We have to get our bikes back. We can't go home without them. And what are we gonna do about Peter Boyle? You KNOW he saw us change.*

I don't know, Rottie-Marin answered as they trotted back, both of them panting hard from the heat and exertion.

Approaching the back of the store, they crept up and took a peek around the corner. Peter was still kneeling in the grass where they left him. Sweat mingled with blood soaked his shirt and shorts. They watched with relief as EMT's carefully wrapped a bandage around his head and placed him on a gurney for transport to the hospital.

While they were watching this, a small van with Jacksonville Animal Control stenciled on its side pulled up next to the dumpsters.

Oh no!. I don't believe it, Rottie-Josh yelled inside Rottie-Marin's head. *They could be looking for us! Run Marin! We've gotta get out of here!* Rottie-Josh and Marin turned and fled from the parking lot at a breakneck speed.

Where do we go? Rottie-Marin thought looking left and right, panicking*. I don't know how much more running I can do today Josh.*

Move it or lose it, Rottie-Josh answered back without any sympathy as he was just as out of breath as Marin. *Follow me. I got an idea*. Rottie-Josh took the lead and led them into the neighboring housing development.

Two oversized Rottweilers could exert a huge force on a door if their lives were at stake. Using their shoulders, they slammed themselves into the side door of an abandoned house. They tried to close the door behind them, but it wouldn't completely close. Frantically looking around, they hunkered down behind a beat up sofa sitting in the middle of the living room.

Do you think we should go upstairs and hide? Rottie-Marin asked looking at the staircase to her left.

No, we need to be able to get out fast. We put a good amount of distance between us and that truck, but we aren't safe yet.

How are we gonna get out fast? We only have one door, Rottie-Marin thought. *I'm getting another bad feeling. Let's look for another way out.*

They got up from their hiding spot and swiftly began investigating the house. As expected, it was dilapidated. There were gaping holes in the walls, floor boards missing on the stairs, and all the windows were boarded up, making it impossible to see out. In addition to the staircase leading up, there were two doors on their level, one leading into the back yard and one probably leading into the basement. After three tries, they gave up. The door leading out wouldn't budge, especially without hands to unlatch the deadbolt.

What do you think? Rottie-Marin asked as they trotted back to the living room. *I want to leave.*

Yeah, let's go. This wasn't such a hot idea.

Poking his head out the side door to look, Rottie-Josh flinched. Waiting on the other side of the door was the dog catcher, wielding a standard six-foot-long catch pole. The man lunged with the pole, using its retractable nylon rope to lasso Rottie-Josh around the neck.

Ahhhh, he's got me! Run Marin! Run! He yelled into her head, the fur uncontrollably standing up on his back. Twisting, turning and pulling, he tried in vain to dislodge the noose around his neck, but it was no good. He was caught.

Rottie-Marin didn't run. *Stop Josh! Don't fight him, you'll only hurt yourself. I got an idea,* she thought. *Just stand there. No better yet, sit! SIT DOWN!* She yelled when he continued to struggle.

Let's see how he likes this, she added as a low growl escaped from her throat. Lowering her head in a gesture of aggressiveness, Marin kept a steady gaze on the man as she slowly approached them.

Listening to his sister, Rottie-Josh stopped fighting and sat down. *Growl*, she thought to Josh. *Growl! Be ferocious and show some teeth! It's two large Rottweiler's against one guy!* Shoulder to shoulder next to Josh, snarling up at his captor, they made their stand.

The man stood gaping at both dogs, unsure of his next move. Rottie-Marin didn't hesitate. She lunged at him. That was all the incentive he needed. Dropping the pole, he turned and fled. Rottie-Marin seized the pole in her mouth before it hit the ground. *Run, she screamed inside his head, run with me!*

They ran.

****

Where do we go now? Rottie-Marin thought, looking around wildly.

I don't know! Rottie-Josh thought. *We are so screwed! We gotta make it home. That shed's our only hope.*

The two of them were trotting single file in the alley that led to their old grammar school, Marin having released the pole. *Keep close to the fence,* Marin thought, letting Josh lead the way. *We don't want any more surprises.*

As they rounded the corner, a minivan came to a screeching stop and blocked their path. Marin and Josh stopped in their tracks. Jumping out from behind the wheel, the driver ran around and flung the side door open.

"You two, get in the van," the woman commanded.

Rottie-Marin and Josh stared at her. If it was possible to display human bewilderment on a dog's face, they did their best to show it. Putting their tails between their legs, they obediently approached the woman.

"Give me that," she demanded reaching for the noose around Josh's neck. Josh held still as the woman slid the lasso from around his neck and angrily snapped the pole in half. "Damn," she said when she saw the mark it had left on Josh's skin.

Jumping inside they saw their bikes stuffed in the back. Marin and Josh collapsed on the seat facing front and rested their heads on their paws, waiting.

"I should have known," she said slipping into the driver's seat. "I should have guessed two weeks ago when Aaron went missing and was suddenly found.. by Danny," she said emphasizing his name and shaking her head. Looking over her shoulder at them she added, "I guess I was in denial. Thirteen is way too young for this."

Chapter 12

Neither kid could see out of the van windows, but they knew where they were, the sound of the garage door opening was too familiar. They were home. Mom pulled the van directly into the now cleaned up garage and closed the door, sealing them inside away from prying eyes. Sliding the van door open, she said, "Come on."

Mom walked over and opened the door that led from the garage to the kitchen for them. Rottie-Josh and Marin once again obediently trailed after her. "Both of you, sit here," she said pointing to a spot in the middle of the dining room. Mom then began to close all of the blinds in the room. "Now each of you focus. I mean, really concentrate on becoming a human. You can do this just as easily as changing into dogs, if you just apply yourselves."

"Close your eyes," she ordered. "That can help a lot. Now, think human…. think human…. think human," she started whispering and chanting for added effect. "Feel your toes wiggle, stretch your arms out, think human…"

Marin was the first to start to change. When she was done, she stood up, walked over and sat down at the dining room table, waiting for Josh. Mom continued coaxing him. It only took a few more minutes for him to join her at the table.

First things first," Mom said. "I'm not mad at you guys. Come over here and give me a hug." Marin and Josh once again obediently got up and joined her in a group hug, the stress of the day lifted by that one action. Tears welled up in Marin's eyes and quietly slid down her face as she held onto her mother and brother.

"I'm sorry," Mom said quietly at last. "I'm sorry that you guys didn't think you could tell me or Dad."

"I'm sorry too," Marin sniffed in reply. "We wanted to, but..." her voice trailed off, leaving the question unanswered.

"I don't know why we didn't tell you Mom," Josh finally uttered. "Maybe we were having too much fun?" he ventured, glancing up at her. "How did you find us?"

"That was a miracle," Marin sniffed, stating the obvious.

"Danny and his dad were at the grocery store. They saw the young man kneeling in the grass, his head bleeding. They stopped to help and called the police. Danny recognized your bikes and called me. I don't think I've ever heard him so upset in my life. Anyway, I pulled up to the store right behind the animal control van and saw you both leaving in a hurry. It didn't take me but a second to figure out what was happening. Two Rottweilers, hanging out together, one with blue eyes...."

"Come over here and sit down, both of you," Mom said as she led them to the couch. "I need to know one thing. You guys didn't hurt that man, did you?"

"No!" They both said simultaneously. Marin continued, "He was attacked by a gang of older boys. We changed to go after them. I really wanted to bite them...but we didn't."

"We just chased them till we got tired. That's all," Josh added adamantly. "We've never hurt anyone. We've been trying to help people...."

"Okay, I believe you. Cause I too have a secret to tell. Can either of you guess what it might be?" she asked with a small gleam in her eye and a bright smile spreading across her face.

"Let me guess," Josh answered excitedly. "You and Dad can both change like we do."

"Close," Mom replied, "very close."

"You can change," Marin guessed. "Just you."

"Correct," Mom said. "But your dad knows all about what we are and what we can do. He's a helper for us," she added, grabbing Josh's hand. "A helper tries to be around us when we change and intervene if something goes wrong. Some of our Society members don't have the ability to change back into a human at will, like you guys can do."

"Huh?" Josh said looking amused. "You told us we could. You practically made us change back."

"What society?" Marin interrupted, her voice trembling with excitement.

"Yeah, I know," she chuckled. "But, I figured you two could do it. You're both way too young for this to have started yet. The norm for us is between 16 and 17." Marin and Josh both looked at each other when she said this, their mouths hanging open. "And not everyone has the same abilities. Some of our members can change only once a month or even less than that. Sometimes the change lasts for over 2 hours and sometimes for as little as ten minutes. It all depends on the person."

"Our first changes lasted for over 2 hours," Marin piped in. "Is that really good?"

"That's excellent, and about the max we can do. Even I don't stay changed that long. I can last about an hour, tops."

"So, what exactly are we?" Josh said, so excited now that he could barely sit still.

Finally answering, Mom replied, "We are an ancient Celtic race of shape shifters called the Púca. Our group is called *The Púca Society* or TPS for short. Here, let me show you something," Mom said as she got up off the couch and went into the den.

Marin and Josh gave each other a knowing look. We were right, Josh wordlessly mouthed to his sister. Marin nodded in reply.

A few moments later Mom came out carrying the book they had found this summer in Marin's room, the one with the giant "P" on it. But she also had a book size magnifying glass in her hand as well. "I found this glass thing in the attic when you guys were cleaning up. Wait till you see this." Opening up the book, she placed the magnifying glass contraption over the names on the last page. Almost like magic, it projected up a handful of names, popping them up like a 3D image a few inches above the page. "See any familiar names?" she asked over her shoulder as she stepped into the adjacent kitchen.

Marin and Josh both stared at it for a few seconds before Josh exclaimed, "Yes! I can't believe I didn't see this before. Your name is here, Mom!"

"It is? Where?" Marin looked at her brother and then back at the projection. "I still don't see her."

"She's right here," he said pointing. "Caitlyn McCray," her maiden name.

"Oh wow! I totally missed that," Marin said with a chuckle.

Mom reappeared after a few minutes with a tray in her hand and placed the contents on the dining room table. "Bring the book over here and sit down. You both need to eat something." Mom had made sandwiches and brought them huge glasses of milk. Both kids dove in at the sight of the food, chugging the milk and inhaling the sandwiches. "I'm going to assume you both have questions, but let me go first. We Púca have a few rules we live by, and you need to learn them, right now."

Rule #1 - We never, ever let anyone see us change.

Rule #2 - We never harm anyone.

Rule #3 - Only violate rules #1 and 2 if someone's life is in danger- yours included.

Rule #4 - Only use your gift for the good of others, never for personal or selfish reasons.

Rule #5 - Eat, rest up, and take care of yourselves or the change will take its toll.

Marin and Josh both continued to eat and nodded as she spoke. "I also have one rule of my own. Learn to communicate with each other nonverbally. This is very important because as you know, once you complete a change, speaking becomes impossible."

Josh and Marin both looked at each other with raised eyebrows. "Uh Mom," Marin said. "How do I say this, umm, we've had a very busy summer?" Mom sighed and plopped down into a seat at the table next to Marin.

"Uh, oh, how busy?" Mom asked, her brow furrowing.

"Really, really busy," Josh answered.

"Oh boy, it's bad enough you guys are way too young for this to have started yet, but what are we talking about here?"

"Um," I started changing at the beginning of the summer. That day, at Jax beach," Marin added in case Mom could have possibly forgotten about her almost drowning incident.

"You did?" Mom looked at Marin with disbelief. "You were in the water. What did you change into?"

"A dolphin."

"A dolphin?" Mom exclaimed, suddenly all excited. "I almost don't believe it. I've never heard of any of us ever changing into a dolphin before. That's extraordinary! And your first change too." Mom sat back with wonderment on her face looking at Marin.

"Well," Marin added trying to explain, "Josh was in trouble. I dove down to help and came up as the dolphin I wished to be at that very moment. I don't remember too much about it though."

"My first time was during our camping trip," Josh spoke up, not to be outdone by his sister. "I found Jack and Jimmy after changing into a wolf. And oh yeah," he added as an afterthought. "We should probably tell you this, but Marin and I can hear each other with our minds when we're animals."

"I'm sorry. What did you say Josh? I don't think I understood you."

"We can hear each other's thoughts when we change," Marin answered for him.

"Once again, I've never, ever heard of this," Mom said shaking her head. "I am going to have the talk to the Society Elders. I am beyond amazed at you two."

"Well, there's more," Josh said and continued on with his story. Both kids took turns during the next hour relating to Mom everything that had happened to them during the summer, up to the day's events with Peter Boyle. "And then you found us," he finished, with a wide yawn. One look at that and Marin mimicked his yawn.

"Okay, up to bed, both of you," Mom ordered, standing up and ushering them upstairs.

"Rule number 5 is rest. We'll talk more about this briefly before school starts tomorrow. I have to update your dad tonight and contact the Elders."

Chapter 13

Marin and Josh both slept fourteen hours that night, the day's exertions having taken their predicted toll. The next morning after both kids had showered and eaten, Dad and Mom sat them down to go over their plans.

"So," Dad started, "Here are our solutions to the problems at hand. Number one, we ignore what happened yesterday. Peter Boyle had a terrible head wound and was practically unconscious when Danny's father found him. No one is going to believe that he saw two kids turn into dogs and chase off that gang."

"Two," Mom continued, "Your friends know your secret and we can't do anything about that. But we need you guys to not let them know that your father and I know your secret too. In fact, we want to you continue on with your lives as if nothing special happened at all this summer."

"We can't stress this enough. And they can't know about yesterday, even though Danny may have guessed. School, swim practices, swim meets, same old normal routine," Dad added.

"Marin, we need you to work on controlling your temper. Josh, we need you to do better with your impulsiveness."

"As for *The Puca Society*, indoctrination is done every three years when we hold a Joining ceremony to welcome the new members. You guys will have to wait until next year to officially be a part of our group. In the meantime, and I can't stress this enough, you are authorized to only practice changing at home, under my supervision or your father. I mean it," she added looking at Marin and Josh, and making sure she had eye contact. "There is no changing without us being here. I don't care if it's to help one of your friends or not."

"What if we see Peter Boyle and he brings it up? I mean, we see him at school all the time. And what about that gang?" Marin asked, her voice hesitant.

"The gang was caught last night. Peter identified the ringleader and they've been arrested on assault charges."

"Awesome," Josh replied, relief in his voice. "Well, at least they didn't see us, only dogs."

"We'll finish this later when you guys get back home from school. Now, hurry up and finish getting ready. The bus will be here in a few minutes."

****

"Amy!" Marin shrieked as she ran to give her best friend a quick hug at the bus stop.

"I can't believe I've been waiting for school to start, just so I could see you!" Amy exclaimed, returning the hug.

"I know. The past two weeks have really sucked. The only consolation is that Josh and I have gotten so much faster with our times. And I am officially way faster than my brother now," she added gloating a bit.

"Do we have any classes together?" Amy asked as they sat down on the bus and started to compare schedules.

"One class and lunch. This bites, but at least it's something. See ya later. We have a lot of catching up to do."

"Yep! See ya later Amy!"

The rest of the morning sped by and Marin found herself in the lunchroom sitting at a table waiting for Amy to join her. Wow, Marin thought, as she looked around the crowded room, where is everybody? Where are all of my friends? There isn't anyone here that I know.

Marin broke into a wide grin, stood up and waved at her best friend when she finally entered the room. Standing right behind Amy, but slightly out of her view was Chris Avery. Marin's jaw dropped and she blushed a crimson shade of red when he returned the wave meant for Amy.

"Oh, my gosh, did you see him behind you?" Marin gushed when Amy sat down next to her.

"See who?"

"Chris Avery was right behind you when you came in. How did you not see him?"

"Cause he was behind me? Why, what happened?

"He waved at me!"

"That's it? I thought maybe he asked you out or something."

"Ha, no, I wish," Marin added with a small sigh. "I haven't really thought about him much this summer."

"Gee, I can't imagine why," Amy answered with a bit of sarcasm in her voice. "It was kinda busy, huh?"

"Yeah, it was," Marin replied quickly and then stopped herself from continuing. Oops, she thought. I just brought up this past summer.

"Hey, did you hear about Peter Boyle?" Amy asked changing the subject. "I heard he got the crap kicked out of him. You should see him. He's in my history class."

Marin and Amy continued chatting while they ate, doing their best to catch up on news. Marin did her best not to bring up the summer's events again. Their lunch period was ending when Marin stood up to empty her tray. Out of the corner of her eye, she caught sight of Peter Boyle approaching their table. "Oh, no," Marin said slowly exhaling. "Amy, we're about to have company."

Amy stood up as Peter Boyle reached their table. "Marin," he said quietly. "Can I talk to you alone?"

Amy had been correct in her description of him. He had a huge bandage that wrapped around his entire head. The area that had been hit was still visibly swollen, giving his head a misshapen shape, like a monster in a horror movie.

"Um...okay," she answered hesitantly looking around. At least they'll be plenty of witnesses if he tries anything, Marin thought as she extracted herself from behind the table. Peter walked over to an adjacent table and sat down. Without him uttering one word, every kid sitting at that table fled from it.

"I want to thank you and apologize," he said slowly, studying her face.

"I don't understand," she replied sitting up straight trying to look taller.

"Yes you do. I told my parents and the police that two huge dogs chased those guys away from me. But I saw what you and your brother did. I know what I saw," he added again, still scanning Marin's face for confirmation that he wasn't crazy.

"I don't know what you're talking about," Marin replied as coolly as she could without emotion, meeting his gaze. "We didn't do anything.

Maybe you were dreaming?" she offered as another explanation, pointing at his bandages.

"I know what I saw," he said again. "Deny it if you want."

Marin tried another tactic in an effort to change the subject away from herself. Shaking her head, Marin confronted him, feeling her temper starting to kick in. "I don't understand you. How can you be such a bully after getting picked on yourself? Are you really sorry Peter? Are you really thankful?"

"Yes, I am," he said, his ears turning a light red. "I want to be friends."

"Friends? Well, friends treat each other better than what you've been doing," she answered, pointing her finger at him.

"I know," he added with remorse in his voice, moving his eyes away from her view. "I'm seeing someone now, someone who can," he added with a slight hesitation, "help me with my anger issues."

Surprised but pleased, Marin said, "Good, then you can start by apologizing to Bobby Lutz and repay him every cent you took from him."

"Oh, okay. I can do that. It may take me a while though."

"I don't think that matters."

BZZZZZ- went the bell sounding the end of the period. Without waiting for Peter to answer, Marin got up and walked over to Amy, a huge grin on her face. "I made a new friend," she said simply as they picked up their trays and exited the cafeteria.

****

"Marin, what the heck happened with you and Peter Boyle today?" Josh exclaimed as they walked to the bus area after school. "It's all over the school," he continued without waiting for her to answer. "He was sitting with you at lunch? Did he threaten you?"

"Nope, nothing like that at all. He apologized and wants to be my friend."

"Wait, what? Friends, with him? Are you out of your mind?"

"Why not? He's sorry he's been a jerk this past year."

"I don't know about you, but I don't trust him."

"There's nothing to trust. He said he was sorry and I believe him." Josh gave her a look that said she must be crazy.

"Did he say anything to you about yesterday?"

"Oh yeah. He says he saw us. But I denied it of course. I mean what else could I say... that he was right?"

"No, but I still don't trust him."

"Listen, he's not stupid, no matter how many times he's been left back. He didn't tell anyone. At least that's what he told me."

"Well, think about it. Who would believe him anyway?"

"True." Marin nodded as Danny walked up to join them.

"Thanks for getting our bikes back," Marin said, giving him a light clap on the back.

"Hey, what are friends for? But really guys, what happened yesterday?" he asked hoping for a juicy answer. "Did Peter Boyle attack you? Did you hit him and that's why you left your bikes there?" Without waiting for an answer from either of them, he continued, "I was dying to call you last night, but knew I would only get you in more trouble."

"No, he didn't attack us. Three other guys attacked him, gang members," Josh answered truthfully. "They picked on him, called him a dummy."

"Wow, so the bully gets bullied. You know my dad told me all about Peter Boyle last night when we got home. He moved here from Orlando last year after his sister died in a car accident. He almost died in that accident too and was in a coma for six months. My dad called it a traumatic brain injury. It's why he sometimes speaks very slowly and why he was left back."

"He's lucky to be alive," Josh admitted feeling a bit ashamed.

"Yes, he is," Marin agreed. "And now he's my friend."

Chapter 14

Mom and Dad were both waiting for them in the living room when they got home. Marin and Josh sat down on the edge of their chairs, nervously waiting for Mom or Dad to start.

"Okay, so here it is. We have good news and we have bad news. I guess we'll start with the bad. We didn't want to have to tell you this until next year, but you need to hear it, especially with everything that happened this summer.'

"I don't know how to say this any gentler, so I'm just going to say it." Drawing a deep breath, she continued, "There is a small group of people called the Eucorach whose sole job it is to hunt us down. They find us, experiment on us, and eventually eliminate us," Mom whispered.

"You mean kill us," Josh said aloud, not really looking for confirmation.

"Yes."

"But I don't understand. Why would anyone do this?" Marin asked.

"Hundreds of years ago, when the first of our kind appeared, we were hated and feared. To utter the name Púca was to be synonymous with evil spirits. The legends say that the "first ones" changed into horses. I'm sure there were some bad apples back then, which is probably how we got the reputation. We don't know. They didn't have the rules we use now to guide us. All we know is that over the years, we Púca eventually evolved."

"Back then, a test of bravery was to go out and hunt us in our changed form. Their job was to stalk us, wound us, but not outright kill us. If one of our kind is killed while in our animal form, we immediately revert back to human form."

"So, they wouldn't kill us outright, because then there wouldn't be any proof of what we were," Josh said.

"Correct. They only needed to incapacitate us. Then they could kill us at their leisure when they had witnesses present."

"And watch us change back as the proof," Marin shuddered.

All of them sat in silence for a few minutes while Marin and Josh digested this.

To break the seriousness of the moment, Marin raised her hand in her mother's direction. "Yes, young lady," Mom said breaking into a small smile. "You have a question?"

"How many Púca are there?"

"There are only a few hundred or so of us scattered around the world," Mom answered. "And to answer what else you might be thinking, you and Josh inherited this from your biological mother. It's passed down from mother to daughter. And just so you know, not everyone passes the gift on to their children, and it's extremely rare for a male child to inherit it. You'll see what I mean at the Joining ceremony next year."

"You can see the lineages there in the book." She added pointing at the book with the gold "P" on it. "I don't know who wrote it, but it's pretty up to date."

"So, what can we change into Mom?" Josh asked.

"Pretty much any kind of animal, and I guess dolphins now too," she added glancing at Marin. "Dogs are the norm though, just in case you wanted to know. Oh, and no insects... but reptiles have been tried before with a little success."

"Could we change into a horse, like you said they did in the old days?" Josh inquired.

"Sure, that's one of our easiest. It's just a bit difficult to get away with, living in a suburb like ours. That always has to be a consideration."

"You also said you had good news too?" Marin asked.

"Yes, it's not really news, just a little more information about our Society." Mom stood up when she said this and slowly started to walk around the room, the teacher in her kicking into high gear. "To be a member of TPS is to be accepted for who you are. At our joining ceremony when we welcome new members, if there are any, we all complete a change to show respect, comfort and trust in, and for each other. We tell the tales of our "First change," we have a little feast, and we remember the fallen." Mom shifted in her seat a bit uncomfortably and continued, "Like your birth parents."

"Our birth parents?" Marin whispered confused. Mom and Dad both nodded.

"You told us they died in a boating accident," Josh added startled, looking from Mom's face to Dad's.

"Yeah, we're sorry we had to tell you that, that but it was for our own safety. You kids were never going to know about the Society."

Marin looked at her mom with hurt in her eyes. "You guys didn't trust us?"

"Sorry honey. There are too many lives at stake. The less people that know about us, the better it is for all concerned." Marin and Josh both looked at each other with a bit of guilt on their faces.

With that, the doorbell chimed and Josh jumped up to get it. Sitting just outside the door was a parcel. "Hey, someone sent me a package," he said as he walked the box inside and put it on the kitchen table to open. Grabbing a small knife, he cut open the box along its seams and ripped the tape off. Peering inside, he gasped and pulled out his backpack. It was the backpack that he had given the boys in the woods that day as a wolf. Taped to the pack was a note. Pulling it off, Josh read it to himself, the tiny hairs standing up on the back of his neck.

"What does it say?" Marin asked as she reached over his shoulder to grab it out of his hand.

Handwritten in red ink were the words, **"They're watching you."**

If you enjoyed this, please visit www.thepuca.com

for news about book two in the series. Thanks!

~Terri Squires

83950158R00135

Made in the USA
Lexington, KY
17 March 2018